(B3T 1/11 16.99)

P9-CRK-681

DISCARD

THREE QUARTERS DEAD

ALSO BY RICHARD PECK

• • •◄○►• • •

RICHARD PECK

THREE
QUARTERS
DEAD

DIAL BOOKS

an imprint of Penguin Group (USA) Inc.

DIAL BOOKS

An imprint of Penguin Group (USA) Inc.
Published by The Penguin Group
Penguin Group (USA) Inc., 375 Hudson Street, New York, NY 10014, U.S.A.
Penguin Group (Canada), 90 Eglinton Avenue East, Suite 700, Toronto,
Ontario, Canada M4P 2Y3 (a division of Pearson Penguin Canada Inc.)
Penguin Books Ltd, 80 Strand, London WC2R 0RL, England
Penguin Ireland, 25 St. Stephen's Green, Dublin 2, Ireland
(a division of Penguin Books Ltd)
Penguin Group (Australia), 250 Camberwell Road, Camberwell, Victoria 3124,
Australia (a division of Pearson Australia Group Pty Ltd)
Penguin Books India Pvt Ltd, 11 Community Centre, Panchsheel Park,
New Delhi - 110 017, India
Penguin Group (NZ), 67 Apollo Drive, Rosedale, North Shore 0632,
New Zealand (a division of Pearson New Zealand Ltd)
Penguin Books (South Africa) (Pty) Ltd, 24 Sturdee Avenue, Rosebank,
Johannesburg 2196, South Africa
Penguin Books Ltd, Registered Offices: 80 Strand, London WC2R 0RL,
England

Copyright © 2010 by Richard Peck
All rights reserved

The publisher does not have any control over and does not assume any
responsibility for author or third-party websites or their content.

Designed by Jennifer Kelly
Text set in Adobe Caslon Pro

Printed in the U.S.A.

1 3 5 7 9 10 8 6 4 2

Library of Congress Cataloging-in-Publication Data
Peck, Richard, date.
Three-quarters dead / Richard Peck.
p. cm.
Summary: Sophomore loner Kerry is overjoyed when three popular senior
girls pick her to be in their clique, until a shocking accident sets off a string of
supernatural occurrences that become more and more threatening.
ISBN 978-0-8037-3454-8 (hardcover)
[1. Dead—Fiction. 2. Friendship—Fiction. 3. Horror stories.]
I. Title.
PZ7.P338Tg 2010
[Fic]—dc22
2009049362

For Trish Marx

THREE QUARTERS DEAD

LIBRARY
HOPKINTON HIGH SCHOOL
CONTOOCOOK, N.H. 03229

PART ONE
Last Fall

ACTUALLY, THIS ISN'T about now. It's about *before*—about last fall, my first semester of sophomore year at Pondfield High School. It's about a lot of lunchtimes. In fact, it's about living for lunch. And it's about one night— Halloween. And a girl named Alyssa Stark, who didn't particularly matter, though she was a senior. This is about last fall when I didn't know who I was or what was coming. It's the time before somebody pulled the world out from under me.

CHAPTER ONE

The Queen of Now

YOU WAIT FOREVER to get to high school. Then you're scared to death. I was. Pondfield regularly makes *Newsweek* magazine's list of America's Top Ten Public High Schools. Even so, my best friend, Abby Davis, went off to boarding school instead. Her parents sent her.

Ninth grade had been in a separate building. It was to keep us from being a bad influence on the middle school people. And to keep the high school people from being a bad influence on us. Whatever.

The point is that I'd washed up at this top school for the top people. Kerry Williamson, a face in the sophomore crowd. Not even. I was so invisible that I was surprised to see myself in the girls' room mirror. And of course I'd turned up in shoes for some other school and a totally wrong T-shirt. I was in everything but Hello Kitty barrettes.

It's funny about time. I can just barely remember those first weeks. September was a blur of phones and backpacks and people who already knew each other. It was everybody in flip-flops that said it was still summer and that school didn't particularly matter, even in AP.

September was all those deafening hallways leading nowhere, and orientation meetings about clubs you didn't want to join.

There was an optional breakout session on Peer Pressure, but I didn't go to that. And they had an assembly on risky behaviors. Little one-act playlets, so I suppose Alyssa Stark might have been in one of them. She was one of the drama people, that semester. Maybe I saw her then.

But she wasn't the kind of senior I noticed. She wasn't strolling in from the parking lot in time for second period. Seniors snapping open their phones to conference, getting a jump on the day, and the teachers. The top seniors in the top school, moving in their separate space. Seniors, still tanned from the beach and backlit by autumn colors. Too cool for school, but running it.

I was two years from senior year, two light-years. I mainly moved in a fog of feeling my way, day by day. Then one day I wasn't alone anymore. Just like that.

I can't put my finger on the exact moment. It was more casual than that, cooler. Now I wish I could remember. Now I rack my brain. But I'd definitely have been having lunch alone. I'd text Abby Davis at her boarding school sometimes just to have somebody to lunch with. But Abby was getting harder to reach. I pictured her in a plaid wool uniform and knee socks, having lunch on a backless bench in a dining hall like a cathedral—Hermione at Hogwarts School. Abby was beginning to fade. People are always gone before you expect it.

Then there at the far end of the lunch table in the food court were Tanya Spangler and Natalie Davenport. Tanya and Natalie, the Ground Zero of senior year, if that's the term. Senior Year Central. There they were, unscrewing the lids off bottles of designer water. And Makenzie Kemp was with them, a junior. In fact she could have ruled junior year if she'd felt like it or had the time.

At first I thought they might be mean—Mean Girls. Not to each other. They were like sisters to each other, but better. But the Mean Girls of seventh grade had sat that close, texting each other across the table, their thumbs flying. They could give you the finger with their thumbs, and all their smiles were sneers. I'd spent middle school keeping out of their way.

But you couldn't even picture Tanya and Natalie and Makenzie ever *being* in seventh grade. Ever. They were like the cast of characters from a TV show about how awesome the teen years are. Tanya, ash blond and completely coordinated—organized beyond belief or reason. Natalie, dark with those double-lashed violet eyes. And more graceful moves than *Swan Lake*. Makenzie with tously hair a color she called "ginger." She was English, or possibly Scottish—whatever—and petite like a little piece of bone china smiling down from a shelf.

They sat there in full color, in a circle of their own private jokes, gusty with laughter, picking at salads, finishing each other's sentences. I could see how it was with them. I had eyes in the side of my head. Natalie was actually the prettiest. Breathtaking, in fact. And Makenzie was the cutest. Not quite life-size, though full of life. But the entire senior class agreed that Tanya was the best looking. Not that I knew any seniors, but she sure looked famous to me.

You could be famous around here even for what you didn't do. And Tanya wasn't running for anything:

senior class president, student senate. Whatever it was, she wasn't running for it. "I don't do politics," she said. "I don't compromise."

I didn't even know what that meant. But I knew what Tanya meant. Natalie wasn't political either, of course. But surely she'd been born to be Homecoming Queen her senior year. That face. That body. Those moves. Who else could you see on a throne with all her court around her, in a tiara right out of *The Princess Diaries*?

Homecoming court was a little bit of a joke and somewhat down-market, even though you got your own double-page spread in the yearbook. But Homecoming Queen or not, Natalie was the most beautiful girl in school. She didn't need a crown or a sash to prove it. She had absolutely nothing to prove.

Still, Tanya seemed to be encouraging her. "Try out for Homecoming Queen, why don't you, Natalie?" she'd say. "You're a shoo-in. And you can pick Sandy Bauer as your escort. You're a little taller than he is, and it'll make you look more regal. Try out for it by all means, *if you want to give it the time*."

But then Natalie realized she didn't. And as Tanya always said, "It's important not to spread yourself too thin."

I didn't know about Makenzie trying out for things. I don't think she ever did. Maybe she'd have been on the prom committee. I don't know. I'll never know now.

But as Tanya said, "Junior year is just basically waiting in the wings for senior year. It's about getting ready. And it's important not to peak early."

Being this close to the three of them at the other end of the table was like sitting at the foot of Mount Everest. I could see the top from here. And even I, two light-years away, felt Tanya's heat warm on my ear. I was *all* ears, eavesdropping to learn the language, to crack the code.

I didn't know why they were even having lunch at school. Why didn't they drive into town for lunch? Seniors had all these ways of not being there. And Makenzie could have ducked out. People probably forgot she wasn't a senior already. I did sometimes.

Not that they were at the table every day. I'd have these dark days when they weren't there. They had committee meetings to sit in on once in a while. But they didn't spread themselves too thin. As Tanya always said, "Don't get overinvolved with people you won't want to know later." She was a real believer in that.

Most days they were there. On my best days, October

days with the world turning red and gold behind them out in the courtyard. Natalie tucking her sensational hair behind her ears. Makenzie swinging her fringed boots just above the floor. Tanya working through her calendar, point by point by point. Running a manicured finger down the page, checking something on her phone. Networking. Multitasking. She didn't text quite as much as you'd think. She phoned, and she wanted you to be there at the other end. They were all three on their phones a lot. Who wasn't?

Even I was, or seemed to be. Even after Abby Davis got too far off and in her world to call me, or call me back, I'd just hold my dead phone to my ear and pretend. I didn't know how to make it ring like somebody was calling me. So I just held it to my ear. How pathetic was that? I know. I know. I probably even moved my lips. But it's what you do when you're fifteen and that far out of the loop.

Who was I even kidding? Who even noticed whether I was on my phone, or the moon?

Actually, somebody did seem to notice. Maybe somebody saw right through me from the other end of the table. Somebody who never missed a trick. All the way into October I never thought they could see me back, the three of them in their sacred circle. But guess what? I was wrong. Somebody spoke from the other end of the table.

"How would you like to friend us?" this voice said. This voice I knew so well. My turned-off phone jerked away from my ear and dropped in my lap.

"What?" I said. Because it was Tanya's voice. Her warmest one.

The friend thing was a joke, of course. Tanya did very little Facebook and no MySpace. I'd heard her say that "friend" is not a verb.

"Me?" I said. Dumb. Dazed. Dry-mouthed. For the first time I looked at them without sneaking a peek. And Tanya was looking back. She had changeable eyes, and now they were sparkling. Inviting.

"Yes, you, Kerry. Why not come sit with us?"

She knew my name.

She knew everything. I expect she probably knew the phone in my lap was dead as a doornail. She glanced down at it in my lap. Just a quick look. Did she feel sorry for me? I didn't think I saw any pity in that sudden glance. No, there was no pity.

Natalie looked up and smiled at me. Makenzie grinned my way. It was like the first glorious day of some new season. It was the first day of everything, for me.

And from that day on until . . . when, forever? From that day on it was the four of us, two on a side, Tanya and Natalie, Makenzie and—Kerry. It was like a story that jumps straight to a happy ending.

Somehow I was there with them, a deer in their headlights, their dazzle. I never wondered—why me? After all, I'd moved from reality to a reality show, and what could be better?

I hung on their every word, hoping for the day I could finish one of their sentences. It took me a while. They remembered things from last year. They remembered people who were seniors when they weren't. Mindy Cashman, who was world-famous with a trophy across from the principal's office because she'd been a gymnast who'd gone to the Olympics. Tanya remembered her well as a sweet girl with a skin condition, but somewhat driven. I limped along behind their conversations. "Try to keep up, Kerry," Tanya would tease me.

"Yes, Kerry," Natalie would say, "really try."

And Makenzie would only smile her private smile and look away. Maybe she remembered being me. And anyway, if there weren't any followers, where would the leaders be? Maybe I was their stake in the future. I'd be here when they were gone. Something like that.

Now that I was this close, I saw why everybody said Tanya was the best looking. The blond hair definitely worked, and the perfect skin unlike Mindy Cashman's. But it was Tanya's eyes: that gaze. Up her eyebrows would arch—perfect arches, and then that gaze that went right through you to the next thing she wanted. Nobody could ever remember what color Tanya's eyes were. They were changeable, but she wasn't.

I lived for lunch. Suddenly it was *High School Musical 4*, and I was in the chorus. In the back row, but working up my moves. I didn't know how. I didn't know why. I only knew I was there, trying to keep up.

Only lunch mattered, and I couldn't wait to get out of bed in the morning. As my mother said, I seemed to be settling into high school.

Other girls sat near us, as near as they dared. Even seniors, though B-list seniors like Emma Bentley and Samantha Jennings. The cheerleaders had their own table, of course, run by Shannon Grady, who was going to be Homecoming Queen even before she knew she was going to be Homecoming Queen.

And one thing I noticed about Tanya—she kept her lines of communication open with everybody, even when she was keeping her distance. "You never know who you'll need," she said.

—◄○►—

I SUPPOSE THE drama people ate in their own bunch, maybe backstage. I don't remember seeing Alyssa Stark at lunch. But then I probably wouldn't have noticed.

Guys buzzed around our table like crazy. They were there for a glimpse from Natalie's sensational eyes. And a word or two from Makenzie to hear her accent. Makenzie was really hanging on to the accent.

But with guys, it was basically all Tanya all the time. Always guys trying to distract her from her phone to notice them for one measly, magic moment.

I wasn't really that ready for boys. My hair felt funny around them, like it wasn't falling as smooth as Natalie's. And here were all these senior guys swooping their trays, reaching for cool. Even some of the more evolved jocks. Several swimmers like the Brolin brothers. A couple of track-and-field types. And student government leaders like Bob Silverman. Once in a while Spence Myers, who edited the school newspaper and had taken it online: www.pondscum.edu. Once in a *rare* while Spence Myers.

Sometimes I wondered why we didn't see more of Spence. He was so much like Tanya, at least in my head. Spiritual twins or something. Bookends holding up the whole senior class. In any group of guys, Spence was the one you noticed. In any group of girls, Tanya was the only one you saw. On a TV soap they'd be a couple—hooking up, breaking up, getting back together—all the fun stuff in a lollipop-colored world. Why weren't they a couple here in reality? Or were they?

I listened a lot to all the conversation buzzing around our table, whether I could process it or not. SATs were behind them. Now the buzzing boys were talking college: how to put together a great essay to promote yourself to colleges, and how to pad your profile. How to package yourself.

And early admissions. And winter term community service that would look good on your application. Building clinics in Guatemala or Sierra Leone or wherever. Also peer counseling and inner-city tutoring. But more important than all that, the prom. And who'd be giving the A-list after-prom parties.

Tanya wasn't into colleges, though I hadn't noticed that yet. But the prom was a different matter. Juniors give the prom in honor of the seniors. And last year

Tanya was naturally head of the prom committee. She and Natalie were co-chairs, and it was the greatest prom ever. The theme was "Evening in Paris," and Tanya had the ballroom of the Beekman Manor done over like Versailles or somewhere, with crystal Eiffel Towers. And she had the fathers of the juniors parking the cars in tuxedos. Then when the juniors' mothers wanted to help with coat check and serving refreshments, Tanya barred them completely. Evidently it was great. Those seniors were probably still talking about it.

—◀○▶—

NOW, HERE IN October, there was already prom talk about next spring. At the time it seemed that the prom would be the major event of the season.

You weren't supposed to take prom too seriously, but people were giving it serious thought. You didn't even have to have a date. Guys in a bunch could go. Girls in a bunch, as long as everybody understood you had a choice.

If you did go with somebody, you didn't have to be in love with him. It was cooler if you weren't, though it was good if he was in love with you. Who you were on prom night became your final senior statement.

People wondered who Tanya would go to the prom with, if she bothered to go with anybody at all.

"Not Spence Myers," Tanya said, though they'd look perfect together. Blond god. Blond goddess. "We know each other too well."

Which I thought was the most sophisticated thing I'd ever heard in my life. Of course, I didn't know what it meant. If their families were friends or something, that could have been the problem. Tanya put up with very little from family.

"Besides, Spence has some growing up to do," Tanya said. "I'll get back to him later." Which I thought was the second-most sophisticated thing I'd ever heard in my life. Though how much more growing up did Spence Myers need to do? He was writing his optional senior thesis on PACs and GSEs in the last two Congressional elections. What *were* PACs and GSEs? And how much more evolved could Spence get?

Some noons we just had to wait for the guys to go away before we could get back to ourselves. One time Tanya got caught in the crossfire between Noah Brolin and Bob Silverman. They were debating about which was a better backup college, Bucknell or Tufts. Something like that.

Finally Tanya had heard more backup college talk than she needed to hear. "Guys, please," she said. "It's not like you're looking at Harvard or Princeton. Bob, your father went to Brown. He gave them a building. You are so in there." Her eyebrows arched their highest. "And Noah, you and Nate are looking for swimming scholarships. You'll go where the money is. End of story."

This sort of left Bob and Noah just standing there. Tanya could talk guytalk better than the guys. And she put up with very little from them. She was amazing. "Enough with the colleges. We're seniors. Let's *be* seniors," she told them. "Let's live in the moment, okay?"

Because Tanya was definitely the Queen of Now.

But what did we spend all that time talking about when the boys weren't buzzing and butting in? Why can't I remember more? Why can't I live in that moment? I reach for us, and we slip through my fingers. I strain to hear, but we're fading now and farther off. The four of us, our heads close, just out of earshot.

One thing I remember that really impressed me was about prom dresses. The subject came up a lot even in October. Also, who would you shop with for your dress?

"I'll take Joanne," Tanya remarked, and Natalie stared at her.

"Joanne?"

"Why not?" Tanya said. "Not the first round, of course. Not for actually picking the dress. We'll do that first, at Nordstrom. Maybe we could all go into the city and have a look at Bergdorf—do lunch upstairs there. Stay overnight at my aunt's. We'll make the basic dress decision. But then I'll take Joanne back later—let her think she's part of the process."

I wondered as long as I could, then had to ask. "Is Joanne a senior?" I limped along behind as usual, and they all screamed, even Makenzie.

Because Joanne was Tanya's dad's live-in girlfriend. Tanya's parents were divorced. So were mine, but in Tanya's perfect life she lived with her dad. Her mother was an archaeologist. She was always on a dig in Syria, or someplace. I wished my mother was on a dig in Syria, or someplace.

◄○►

THEN THERE WERE other noons when the girls were too busy for much talking. They'd be texting the questions on some Algebra II or science test from that morning for people in the afternoon class. "It's my take on community service," Tanya said. "It's not like we owe the afternoon people anything in particular. But we have to keep some control over the teachers. Really, the way they make us grovel for grades. Honestly, who do they think they are? Could they even *get* real jobs in, like, business?"

Tanya put up with very little from teachers.

◄◦►

SO I SUPPOSE I actually remember quite a lot about those noons, and what was said. What Tanya said. But surely there was more to the code than I ever cracked. Moments I missed. Clues. An hour here, an hour there, now gone forever.

There's one thing I almost noticed. Lunch at Tanya's table sometimes seemed to go on longer than regular time. Of course the bell at the end always went too soon, right in the middle of a sentence, which was annoying.

But for lots of lunches, time just seemed to stand still, the clock locked at high noon. The rest of the food court and school, and the world, kind of fell away. It was funny. Odd. We hung there in Tanya's special space, this island in time, because she said so. She really, truly was the Queen of Now.

But then came that miracle noon I hadn't even dared to hope for. It was the last golden day of October, and all three of them turned to me. Me. Just like that.

They'd been talking about Halloween. Their own take on Halloween. I couldn't picture them going door to door, holding out their little plastic jack-o'-lantern pails. Anyway, I'd never been included in anything but lunch. I had the idea they thought maybe I wasn't quite ready for . . . prime time.

But then Tanya turned to me, like I'd been on her agenda all along. From that day she'd overlooked the phone in my lap and drew me with her eyes into the group. "Tonight at my house, Kerry? Just dessert and coffee. Decaf. Then we'll see where the evening takes us." Just like that.

Me? Time really did stand still then, like my heart. And the countdown till tonight started ticking. They'd decided on jeans and bulky sweaters.

"What a pity," Makenzie said. "I can still get into my old Tinker Bell costume."

CHAPTER TWO

The Picture of Alyssa

BEFORE MY PARENTS' divorce, we lived so near Tanya's house I could have walked up there. Now my mother had to drive me. Which I didn't particularly like. But anything to get there. Halloween was already happening all over town.

Some people went a little overboard on the house decorations. Life-size scarecrows beside doors and floodlit ghosts escaping from dormer windows and plastic tombstones on lawns, reading REST IN PIECES. Fake cobwebs by the ton.

It was still the kiddy time of evening. The crosswalks were crowded with parents and nannies leading tiny trick-or-treaters. Little Brides of Frankenstein and one Snow White after another. Dinosaurs and flop-earred Eeyores. Mini-mummies unraveling along the pavement. Small, toddling Draculas with their black tailcoats sweeping the pavement behind.

Waiting for a light, my mother said, "Remember the year you wanted to be the Little Mermaid?"

"Turn left at the top of the hill," I said, because you could almost see Ridge Road from here.

The Halloween decorations were all professionally done. Not an artificial cobweb in sight. Nothing floodlit. Only a few front lights were on to welcome trick-or-treaters. Now we were at Tanya's, because Natalie's Audi and Makenzie's Scion were parked out by the curb.

"Don't turn in the drive," I told my mother.

"I have to turn around," she said. "Call me when—"

"I'll get a ride home." I was out of the car already, heading up the curving flagstone walk over all that rolling lawn, not a leaf fallen on it. Not a plastic tombstone. It was a long, rambling house, country French, probably. At the entrance was an arrangement of squashes and gourds and ears of corn in designer colors. A florist had done it. Very restrained.

I rang the bell, and lights flickered inside, through the leaded-glass window of the door. A tall, willowy figure was coming closer, a silhouette. I wanted it to be Tanya, but when the door opened, it was a really thin, really glamorous woman in a white turtleneck sweater.

"You must be Kerry," she said. "I'm Joanne."

She led me through the fabulous house, up a step, down a step, over Oriental rugs glowing in dark reds and blues on polished floors. If you were going to imagine the house Tanya would live in, here it was. We moved toward warm light and laughter. It wasn't the formal dining room. It was another one, and I could see them from here, around the table: busy at something, leaning over to each other, being in their zone.

And here was the great part. They were all three wearing these towering, black, pointy witch hats: black felt with wavery brims and half as tall as the room. It was great. They were.

Joanne turned just at the door. "Watch your back," she murmured. But I looked behind me, and there wasn't anything there.

—◄○►—

THEN IT WAS the four of us. "Here's Kerry finally," Tanya said, though I was on time. "Joanne, you can bring in the dessert now."

They were sitting around this table in their witch hats, she and Natalie and Makenzie, and I'll never forget one thing in particular. Laid out on the table in two neat rows were miniature black coffins. Nine of them. Little coffins with handles. The rest of the table was littered with orange and black ribbon, note cards, little parchment scrolls like tiny diplomas, rolls of tape. All kinds of stuff, but the little coffins were what I really noticed, after their hats.

When I'd sat down, I saw the coffins were gift boxes of Belgian chocolates, from Neiman's. The three of them were dressing up the boxes even more, tricking them out with black bows. Makenzie was writing on a little scroll.

"It's our annual Halloween Hotties award for the top ten senior guys," Tanya said. "A tradition."

"Which we've just started this year," Natalie said.

Makenzie sat on her foot, carefully lettering away, busy as a bee.

They put me to work on the name tags. Then Natalie tied them onto the coffins with orange and black ribbon and little grinning pumpkins on pipe cleaners:

Liam Buckley   Austin Zeller
Ben Chou   Grant Carmichael
Sandy Bauer   Sasha Cole
Bob Silverman   Nate and Noah Brolin
Chase Haverkamp

They decided to give Nate and Noah Brolin a joint award. Tanya said that as individuals, they didn't quite make the grade. And Nate was seeing a girl from some other school. Greenwich, people said. So Tanya thought Nate wasn't really committed to Pondfield. But being identical twins added interest, and Nate and Noah were co-captains of the swim team.

Makenzie lettered a special card for the Brolin brothers:

Halloween cheers
And Halloween yelps
Put the two of you together
And, voila—Michael Phelps!

"Cute," Tanya said, but there wasn't time to make a special rhyme for everybody. The rest got citations on little scrolls, reading:

Congratulations for being
a Halloween Hottie,
One of 10 and 10 only Pondfield
Senior guys as judged by
4 Classy Witches

Four.

I saw that, and my eyes stung. Was I one of them, one of four classy witches? They watched me see that. Tanya did. Her eyes reeled me in. Once again it was like a story that jumps to a happy ending.

Now Tanya was reaching down under the table to bring up another witch hat. For me. She handed it over the table. So I thought, this is it. I'm in the magic circle. I wasn't quite, but I thought I was. Makenzie glanced up at me in the hat, then back down at the scroll she was finishing. And there we sat, with our tall black hats pointing at the ceiling, and the future.

"I know, I know," Tanya said. "The Hotties thing is a little bit ditzy. It's a little like Shannon's cheerleaders poking all that crepe paper into a homecoming float. But it's for a good cause. Guys love awards—remember all those Cub Scout badges? They like their gold stars. It's not that much work for us, and it helps with their self-esteem."

Also it meant that the guys didn't decide who was top ten. Tanya did. If I'd noticed that, I'd have thought it was great.

Somewhere in all this Joanne brought in the dessert and a silver pot of coffee.

"She won't be joining us," Tanya said when Joanne

was barely back in the kitchen. "Eating disorder. The only way you can be that thin at her age is to keep sticking your finger down your throat."

"Gross," Natalie said as Makenzie reached for the bowl of whipped cream for the pumpkin pie. She was our heartiest eater, but Natalie was always hungry.

"Is your dad dating again, Kerry?" Tanya said, out of the blue. She could catch you off guard every time. You never saw Tanya coming.

Dating again? How did she even know my parents were divorced? But then, she knew all kinds of things about adults. She practically was one.

"No, Dad's not dating," I said.

"Don't be too sure," Tanya said. "They always start sooner than you think. And they always go for somebody younger. And younger. And younger, till they're practically your age." She looked at the kitchen door. "Or think they are."

She held up the silver pot. "How do you take your coffee?"

And of course I didn't know how I took coffee.

"The best thing about you, Kerry, is that nothing ever happened to you before you met us," Tanya said. "You don't have to be retrained."

—◀○▶—

I REMEMBER NOW how that part of the evening seemed to go on longer than it could have. And the little black candy coffins and the pumpkin-shaped gift bags we were going to deliver them in: orange and green foil with handles to hang on doorknobs. I saw that far. We'd drive all around town, delivering the coffins to the Halloween Hotties' houses. We'd be going in Natalie's Audi because Makenzie's GPS had a bug in it.

Then when we were slipping the coffins into the pumpkin bags, I realized something. I don't know why.

"Isn't Spence Myers a Halloween Hottie?" I said, surprised. "How come he's not on the list?" He was surely up high in anybody's top ten. Editor of the newspaper and into a lot of things. Triple 800s on his SATs. I wasn't sure what that meant, but it was good. And the looks. He so had the looks.

Makenzie and Natalie watched Tanya, waiting.

"We're talking really just top ten, Kerry," she said, explaining, patient. "Spence isn't quite there yet. He falls a little short. Let's think of these not only as awards to the top ten, but as an incentive to others, maybe to work a little harder, like take closer looks at themselves.

"You know how un-self-critical guys are. They really do let themselves off too easy. You see?"

I guessed so. But not really. Besides, there was more to the evening. Another part of the . . . agenda.

◄○►

I THOUGHT WE were ready to go. But Tanya was looking for something among the coffee cups and clutter. For once she wasn't holding me with her gaze. "Where's the baby?" she said.

Baby?

But she must have known, because she reached under some ribbon ends and held up something. It was a plastic baby doll, three or four inches high. Naked and too pink. Like something from the dollar store. Natalie was watching me, and Makenzie was looking away. I think so. I was mainly staring at this cheapo little doll that looked all wrong for the room.

Tanya held it up to the light, and there was a line of red across its neck and a drop or two of red, like blood. Maybe nail polish. It was the first really eerie moment of Halloween.

The room got too quiet, so I said, "What's that an award for?"

"You could think of it as an award, I suppose," Tanya said.

"Please," Natalie murmured.

"You really could." Tanya came up with a plain little cloth bag with a drawstring top. She slid the plastic doll into it, up to the bloody neck, and drew the drawstring tight.

"Kerry, you're going to deliver this one personally to a girl named Alyssa Stark. Think of it as kind of a joke thing. We don't have time to go into it. Let's just say it's a long story, and Alyssa has this coming to her."

Me? "Me?"

"Yes," Tanya said. "Kind of an initiation type thing."

"You mean like initiation into a sorority?" I said, not really getting it.

Natalie sighed.

"Well, sororities are kind of tacky," Tanya said, "unless you're pledging Kappa at the University of Virginia. That sort of thing. Let's just say this is something you can do to make yourself a part of us. You have something to decide, Kerry. When we pull up the drawbridge, which side of the moat do you want to be on?"

We sat there, and all I could see in my mind were drawbridges being pulled up. Tanya's hand rested on the table beside the doll in the drawstring bag, looking at the ceiling with its pinpoint eyes. Makenzie was a little pulled back from the table. I wondered if she'd had to do something to prove herself.

But Tanya was saying, "Makenzie, get a picture of this with your phone in case we want to e-mail it to everybody. We'll have that option." And Makenzie was scavenging around for her phone.

I really didn't know where this was going. Just for a moment I wished I was home, in bed. But the moment passed. We had to get busy. We had all these coffins to deliver in the right order. Alyssa's award was going to be the last.

"I have a black sweater that will be better for you, Kerry," Tanya said. My only bulky sweater was Christmas red. The wrong color of course. She had the sweater ready too, under the table. "Black will help you blend in with the night."

All she had to do was hand it over. All I had to do was take it.

◄○►

SURELY WE'D SAT around that table for hours. The remains of the whipped cream were dry in the bowl and at the corners of Makenzie's mouth.

Then we were hours more, driving all over to leave the awards at the guys' houses. The night was velvet. Moonless. Most of the porch lights were out since it was past the trick-or-treaters' bedtimes. The crosswalks were empty.

We drove through every curving street up at this end of town. Chase Haverkamp lived on an estate. You couldn't see the house from the road. You couldn't get past the gate. We had to leave his coffin on the doorknob of the gatehouse. I didn't know where Spence Myers lived. We didn't go there.

We'd had to give up our witch hats. They didn't fit in the Audi. Makenzie and I took turns darting out of the backseat of the car to leave the awards. We didn't buckle up. How could we? We were in and out. Natalie drove, and Tanya sat up front beside her, checking off the addresses on the list by the light of a little pen flashlight. Organized. It was fine. It was fun. But I was getting a little worried. Something was gnawing at me.

Then finally, finally we'd delivered all our coffins. Natalie was turning down the hill to another part of town. She was a cautious driver, always with the turn signal, careful not to attract a cruising village cop car.

We were down low in the town, several blocks below where I lived. We turned on Harper Street, which was a line of tired little ranch type houses, from the 1950s or whenever. Picture windows. A lot of unraked leaves. The Metro-North railroad tracks ran right behind. A city-bound train rumbled through as we made the turn.

The Audi crept along the street where nothing stirred at this hour. The witching hour. Natalie killed the lights and coasted into the curb, mashing leaves. She killed the engine. We sat in the dark for a moment or two. "Here's the baby. Put it in your pocket. Keep both hands free." Tanya handed it over her shoulder to me. I saw the shape of it coming toward me, the doll in its little sack, in Tanya's hand. Makenzie sat there in the back beside me, still as a statue, separate. I took the doll, though I really didn't want—

"And here's the key." Tanya handed it back.

The key.

"It's to the front door."

"I have to go inside?" I went cold all over.

"Yes," Tanya said in her evenest voice. "You'll be fine. Alyssa's in the city tonight, and her mother works a late shift. There is no father."

"I have to go inside?" Me? Into some strange house?

"Yes," Tanya said. "You've got the key. You're not breaking in. And look—nobody's around, and it's dark as pitch except for the streetlight. If anybody did see you going up to the house, they'd just think it was Alyssa coming home. She's always out all hours. Or her mother. And anyway, who's to see?"

"But what do I do when I get inside?"

"Well, for a start, you don't turn on a light."

I couldn't breathe. Or believe this. And I couldn't picture myself in somebody's dark house with all the furniture around like shapes. And what about burglar alarms? Every house up on Ridge Road had them.

"I can't—"

"The front door opens right into the living room. All these houses are the same. Very simple layout." Tanya seemed to be speaking straight ahead, not over her shoulder. But I heard. I heard. "Two bedrooms with a bath between," she said. "Turn left out of the living room. Then left again, and you're in Alyssa's bedroom. She's got the front one. There's a ceiling light, but don't turn it on. You can see enough from the streetlight out here."

"But what am I supposed to do?" I was trying not to whine. But what was I supposed to do?

"Nothing, really. Just take the doll and put it on the pillow of the bed. Right there where she'll see it as soon as she comes in and turns on the light. Who knows? She may not be back till morning. Then she'll find it."

"But what's the point?" I said. "I don't get it."

"I know you don't," Tanya said. "Think of the whole thing as a treasure hunt."

Natalie sighed.

"A treasure hunt," Tanya said. "Except you'll be leaving something, not taking something."

Silence sort of fell. Was I waiting for her to change her mind?

"And the sooner you go, the sooner you'll be back."

I pushed open the door. A night breeze scudded the leaves along the sidewalk.

"It's the third house back," Tanya said, low. "Count back three houses." So they hadn't parked in front of Alyssa's house. That made sense, I supposed.

"Where's the key?" Tanya said.

"In my hand."

"Don't drop it. You'll never find it again in all these leaves. Don't these people ever rake?"

The car door closed behind me with only a click.

I was a little dizzy out here, and the wind had turned colder. My feet barely found the sidewalk. But I was walking now, blending with the night in Tanya's black sweater. I had the key in a death grip. I could feel the doll in my jeans pocket. The houses were close. Now I was in front of the third one. I looked back once at the dark car by the curb, and it seemed miles away.

There wasn't much to the front yards. I was already on a concrete step, up to a front door. The storm door was loose, shuddering in the wind. I held it open with an elbow while I found the lock with the key. There was just enough light.

And I thought, just for a moment: *I'm on my own here. I can still back out. I can make this not happen.* But the moment passed, and the key slid right in. I turned it, and I was ready to run—poised—in case of a burglar alarm. But no bells rang except maybe in my head. I had to go on, and now I was inside, closing the door behind me. It was two or three shades of dark in here. The furniture was just one shape after another. For a moment I couldn't tell up from down. Then I saw an opening into blackness, a door on the left that went to the bedrooms and the bathroom. I went that way like a sleepwalker, careful not to run into anything or touch anything. Maybe I wasn't there at all.

Now I was in this little hallway area that closed in on me. I needed to turn left again. I couldn't see my feet, so it was like walking through leaves, but quieter. The door to Alyssa's bedroom was open, and there was some light from outside. Pale silvery light fell across the bedspread.

I was in this girl's bedroom, and I didn't really know who she was. I didn't know her. But there was this jumble of little things on a chest of drawers. And shapes. All these shapes. I fumbled in my pocket for the doll. Then I fumbled in the other pocket where the doll really was, shifting the key from hand to hand.

I had the doll now. The baby. All I had to do was leave it on the pillow. Right where she'd see it. My hand tingled to get rid of it.

I put it there, not touching the pillow, and turned.

And then: "Alyssa?" someone said.

My feet froze to the floor. Light flooded the room. The ceiling light was on, and this woman was standing in the door to the dark hall. A woman in a bathrobe, clutching the collar of it at her throat.

"You're not Alyssa." She stepped back. She'd been asleep, and now she wasn't.

Somewhere outside a car started up and gunned away over the mashed leaves.

"Who are you?" she said. Alyssa's mother said. "What are you doing here? Why are you in this house?"

Good question.

"I said, who are you?"

I was terminally terrified. I could hear my heart. It was about to jump out of Tanya's sweater.

"Kerry Williamson," I said. I'd have told anything. I'd have shown her ID if I had any. And how could I run? She was standing there in the only door.

She'd heard me come in the house. She was somebody's mother, so she woke up the instant she heard the key in the door. It was a wonder I hadn't walked right into her in the little dark hall.

"I'm in tenth grade," I said.

It was an insane thing to say. What did I mean? Was I trying to say that I was only in tenth grade, so I wasn't responsible for anything? That it wasn't like I was a senior? I don't know why I said that. I was crazy and too scared to cry.

"Why?" Alyssa's mother said. She'd put on her

glasses, and her hair was a mess, and her nose was red and runny. Suddenly I knew. She had a cold, so she'd called in sick, and that's why she wasn't at work. I could figure all that out. I just couldn't figure out why I was here.

"What's that on the pillow?"

"A doll," I heard myself saying. "I've brought it for Alyssa." That almost sounded like a reason, or so I thought after I'd said it. An excuse.

She wasn't scared of me now. Anyway, she'd heard the car drive away just as I had, the Audi. The minute the ceiling light went on, the car cut out. She knew I was alone.

"Give it to me." She put out her hand. She was this mother, so I had to do it. If I behaved, maybe she'd just let me go or something. Maybe we could just make this be—not happening. I picked up the doll and handed it over.

It rocked in the palm of her hand under the glaring light. The little bag had fallen off, so it was this fairly nasty small slick pink thing in her hand. She'd have seen the fake blood on the slit neck.

"What is this supposed to mean?" The light glinted off her glasses. She looked so tired, and I was so tired.

"I don't know what it means," I said. Mumbled.

"Then why did you bring it here?"

"It's Halloween," I said, remembering that it was. "It's just like a Halloween type thing."

"And how did you get in here?"

I held out the key.

She was so surprised she didn't even take it. Then she took it. "How in the world did you get this? Did Alyssa give you a key? Do you know her?"

I thought about saying yes, but Alyssa could walk in the door this minute. She was always out till all hours, and it was all hours.

"I don't even know who she is," I said, "exactly."

Mrs. Stark stared at me, trying to make some sense out of this.

"She's a senior," I said, but then, her mother would know that.

"Did you steal this key?" Mrs. Stark said. "Somebody did."

"No. Tanya gave it to me." I blurted that out before I thought. Still, they'd left me here. They'd dropped me in this. Didn't they care? No, they didn't.

Now Mrs. Stark was wide awake. "Tanya Spangler?" she said. "That could explain almost anything."

Could it?

She was stepping aside, though it was too late to run for it. She knew my name.

"I'm just going to tell you one thing," she said. "And you're not going to understand it."

We were close, there in that little room. But I waited and listened and almost looked at her. If I did everything she wanted me to, maybe she'd let—

"You're being used," she said. Whatever that meant.

And was that it?

No. No. She walked me out through the living room and flipped on a light. The room came alive with colors.

A picture hung by the door. I caught one glimpse of it, a framed photograph of a girl. Not as pretty as Natalie. Not as great-looking as Tanya, but dramatic. Maybe a little older. Alyssa? I didn't recognize her. I didn't recognize a lot of people. It was a big school, and you couldn't know everybody, and it was important not to get involved with people you wouldn't want to know later.

My head was spinning out of control, but the door was right here, a reach away. Mrs. Stark was behind me. I could feel her there, all the way down my spine. But she didn't touch me, hold me back. She was leaning around me to open the door, and I was *this close* to freedom, to blending with the night.

Then she said, close to my ear, "You're Carolyn Williamson's daughter, aren't you?"

And that broke me. Into pieces. It broke me apart. She knew my mother.

Chapter Three

Blending with the Night

I RAN, KICKING through the leaves, up one street after another. It was like running in a nightmare. Running and running, and are you even moving?

For a crazy moment I thought about going to my dad's instead. I was with him part of the time, once in a while. I was back and forth, so why not now? He had an apartment in White Plains, and I could double back to the station and take the next train. Be there for breakfast.

But I didn't have any money, so I just kept running, numb all the way home. A car turned ahead of me under a streetlight. In case it was a police cruiser I jumped into a bush with branches like claws.

I was on Linden Street before I knew it. We lived in

the Groveland, a big old apartment building that had gone condo. It was on the edge of the Old English Village part of town.

Now I was walking, breathing in heaves, almost home. I'd brought my keys. I was well supplied with keys that night. So I could get into the lobby downstairs. The front door snapped shut behind me. On the long table a big bowl still held some Halloween candy. The usual fake fire glowed in the lobby fireplace.

I took the elevator up, and my door key was in my hand. The morning paper was already on our mat. I left it there. I didn't even look down. I didn't want to see some headline reading:

LOCAL TENTH GRADER NABBED IN . . . I didn't know what . . . NABBED IN DISTRIBUTING DOLLS TO PEOPLE'S BEDROOMS.

Besides, if I left the paper on the mat, it would mean I'd come home earlier, before it was delivered. I turned the key in the lock, quiet as a mouse.

Inside, I could see my bedroom door from here. At the end of the hall. But this was the trickiest part. I had to walk past my mother's bedroom door.

And a line of light was under it. A bright fan of light across the dark hall floor. My flesh crept.

Her light was on, but I wasn't about to knock and turn myself in. It had to be nearly daylight. Why wasn't it? She shouldn't see my face. Who knew what she'd be able to read in it?

I kept walking on little mouse feet, past her door. Then I was in my room, on the safe side of the door.

I nearly lost it then. But I was home free, maybe, and maybe my mother had gone to sleep, waiting for me. She must have. The most important part was that Mrs. Stark hadn't called her. And Mrs. Stark knew her. How? But she did.

I don't remember any more about that night. I must have tried to stay awake as long as I could, so I'd be ready for my mother if she barged in. But then I slept, hard and fast and friendless. Then it was the next day, a school day. About an hour later.

And I don't think my mother had come into my room. But had I folded up Tanya's sweater that neatly? And left it on the chair to remember to take it back to her?

—◁◦▷—

I WASN'T EVEN late for school, though still numb. But I remembered to stuff Tanya's sweater into my backpack.

I meant to throw it at her and walk away. She'd walked away from me. Worse.

Then all morning I kept looking around at these people in my tenth-grade classes. Geometry and whatever. They weren't real, and lunch was. Were these the people I was stuck with now? Now that Tanya and Natalie and Makenzie had dropped me in it? And probably dropped *me*? And didn't care?

Kimberly Cook was tenth-grade class president. There she was in second period, though I didn't particularly know her. And the guys were all so immature. There were some very recent voice changes in some of them. And a Mets sweatshirt on one of them. It was whole classrooms full of the clueless. Whole bunches of wannabes who didn't even know who they wanted to be. I knew.

I dreaded lunch. I wanted to stop all the classroom clocks, which was a new feeling. Then I thought about not going to lunch at all. I could throw Tanya's sweater at her some other time. Why hadn't I brought an energy bar or something? But my feet took me to the food court. I went through the salad bar and dropped down at the far end of the usual table, the end where I used to sit alone, before.

Nothing tasted like anything, and I was invisible, and it was September again: that thundering buzz of everybody knowing everybody else. Everybody locked in.

I decided that if they came to lunch, they'd find me on my phone. It would be like an IM had just popped up on my screen. Maybe from Abby Davis, though I hadn't heard from her in a month. I decided how to act. Then they were there, and my phone wasn't even in my hand.

They swept up and dropped down around me like birds. Chattering birds on a branch here at this end of the table. With their designer water and low-carb salads. And Tanya and Natalie were wearing pajamas.

Pajamas? I was mad at them, and they were wearing pajamas? As usual, I was way behind, and they were way ahead.

The pajamas were a senior thing, a cross between some fund raiser and a protest against first period. Natalie was in shortie pajamas with a body stocking underneath and heels, black patent leather. She looked sensational. Like a French movie or something. Tanya was wearing her father's pajamas, rolled up: maroon stripes, and over that a floaty dressing gown you could see through. It was perfect. She'd tied up her blond hair in hanks with flannel strips and cold-creamed her face. A hoot.

The floaty gown settled around her as she settled next to me. "Do you love it?" Tanya said, holding out a see-through sleeve. "It's Joanne's. Her sleepwear and undies are very Victoria's Secret. She has *garter belts*. Did you get home all right?"

Did I get home all right? I couldn't believe my ears.

"Don't sulk," she said. "It makes you even younger."

"It really does," Natalie said. "I'm thinking training bra and braces."

Tanya couldn't get the lid off her water and handed it to Natalie to unscrew. "Honestly, when the light went on in Alyssa's bedroom, we had to leave," Natalie said, nearly looking at me. "You were so busted, Kerry. I mean, you walked right into it. And it was bound to be Mrs. Stark, so how did we know she wouldn't go psycho and dial 911? Police? *Please.*"

They all three looked at me. I was the center of attention.

"It was Mrs. Stark all right," I mumbled. "She had a cold or something. And she knows my mother."

Makenzie's big eyes got bigger. She needed glasses, but they were almost always parked up in her hair. She wasn't in pajamas, not being a senior. She was in one of her kilt type outfits. A touch of tartan.

Tanya hardly missed a beat. "Well of course she knows your mother. Why wouldn't she?"

Why would she?

"Mrs. Stark works in the admissions office at the Crossland Hospital ER. She checks people's health coverage."

Oh. But so what?

Tanya waited for me to figure it out, then gave up. "Your mother used to do volunteer work at Crossland Hospital, before the divorce." Tanya always had adults so nailed. "Kerry, adults have their networks too. Don't you know that?"

"I know that," I said. Actually, I didn't. I tried to keep my parents in these little boxes, separate from me and everything. Now I was getting confused and not as mad as I'd meant to be.

"She wanted to know where I got the key," I said. "Mrs. Stark did."

Natalie sighed one of her sighs.

Tanya was working the wrapper off of two little rounds of melba toast. "Alyssa needs to be more careful about where she leaves her backpack."

She and Natalie both skimmed a glance over Makenzie. But Makenzie was gazing away at some other table, with her glasses on now.

And I saw right then. Makenzie had stolen the house key out of Alyssa's backpack. The drama people leave their stuff backstage in the theater area. I could picture Makenzie, small and quick, kilted. She'd have been in and out before anyone saw, with Alyssa's key pressed in the palm of her hand. She could have pulled off the whole thing on a restroom pass.

Maybe it had been Makenzie's initiation. Maybe there was no end to the initiations.

It had to be Makenzie. Tanya didn't steal things. She delegated.

"Mrs. Stark wanted to know what the doll was about," I said. "She made me hand it to her."

"Oh dear, I hope she doesn't keep it from Alyssa." Tanya balled up her napkin. "I hope Alyssa sees it." Natalie was taking her tray back, so Tanya pushed hers across to her.

"*Why* does Alyssa have to see it?" I was trying not to whine. I didn't want to be a whiner.

Makenzie was still drifting, still staring off somewhere. Natalie was taking the trays back.

Tanya held me in this small space of the two of us. Like we were both in a little drawstring bag, pulled tight. "Kerry, Alyssa was absent from school for a couple of days early last month. Two consecutive days. Liam Buckley knows how to hack into the school's records. Okay? So we have hard copy on this. Documentation."

People are absent all the time. Especially seniors.

"What does her attendance record matter?" I said. Or should I be able to work this out for myself?

"It's *why* she was absent," Tanya said, very low, very quiet. It was just the two of us in this deafening, tray-banging room.

"Why was she absent?" I asked because I was supposed to ask.

"She had a . . . procedure, Kerry. An outpatient procedure. Not at Crossland Hospital, of course. Somewhere else. Maybe in the city. Maybe Jersey. It doesn't matter where. It really doesn't."

I didn't get it.

"Kerry, do I have to spell it out for you? When Alyssa went in for the procedure, she was going to have a baby. When she came out of the procedure, she wasn't. Okay?"

I knew what she was talking about. It wasn't a word I

was used to, but suddenly I saw the slick little pink doll with the slit—

"Is that what it said on her absence excuse? Did Liam Buckley find—"

"No, of course it didn't, Kerry." Tanya sighed one of Natalie's sighs. "The excuse was totally something else. Totally bogus. Outrageously bogus. It doesn't even matter."

"Why does it matter to—us?" I asked her.

"Kerry, think. Alyssa did something very wrong; she needs to be reminded of it everywhere she turns. Even her pillow. You know, people really have their heads in the sand about Alyssa. And if we have to get the word out about her, we will."

The bell was about to ring, and I didn't know what to think. And I ought to be bright enough to know all there was to know about Alyssa Stark. Somehow I'd made her my business. How had I done that?

"What will she do now?"

Tanya brought up her silken shoulders, turned up her manicured hands. "Who knows? But if everybody finds out what she is, I doubt if she'd want to stay in school. Would you? The best thing for her is if she just graduates at the end of this semester. It'll be better for the school. According to her transcript, she has enough credits to graduate early. Liam has hard copy on it."

One more jump of the clock, and the bell would ring. Except it didn't. Tanya could stop time, letting me think, except I couldn't.

"And of course there's more to the story," Tanya said. "Isn't there?"

More?

I could feel her arm, smooth against mine. We were that close. "Like who's the father?" she said, softly.

"Who is?" I said.

Tanya shrugged him off, whoever he was. "Could have been a lot of people. But I think it's pretty obvious."

Not to me it wasn't. But Tanya left me hanging. She was good at that. Awesome.

The clock was one jump from the bell. "How are you dealing with your mother?" Tanya asked.

My mother? Oh.

"Her light was on when I got home. But she didn't say anything this morning." And I'd skipped breakfast. She'd been at her computer before I left for school. "I think she went to sleep before I got back."

"I think she was awake," Tanya said, "waiting."

"Why?"

"Because Mrs. Stark would have called her. She wouldn't just send you off into the night. I'm surprised she didn't call your mother to come and get you."

My flesh crept. My spine tingled.

Yes, Mrs. Stark probably did call my mother. That's why the light was on in her room. She was waiting for me to come home.

"Don't let her make an issue out of this," Tanya said. "Be as firm as you need to be. Remember, she has no say in what you do and who you are. Why should she? Your mother couldn't even hold her own marriage together."

By now we'd forgotten all about why I was in Alyssa Stark's bedroom to begin with. The clock jumped, and the bell rang. I needed to take my tray back.

"Kerry, have you forgotten something?" Tanya said.

No. Maybe. "What?"

"My sweater?"

Oh yes, her sweater. I had planned to throw it at her, right in her face. But then I forgot to give it to her.

—◄❍►—

SO WE WERE lunching again, and I needed to get over myself. I zoomed back into their zone. In fact I'd never left. And the main thing people remembered about Halloween was the Halloween Hotties award business. There was a lot of buzz about that: who had made the cut, who hadn't. Liam and Sandy wore the black and orange ribbons on their shirts at school, like medals, making the point but keeping it light.

Then people moved on to homecoming, which was late that year. Since Natalie hadn't wanted to be Homecoming Queen, Shannon Grady was, with her cheerleaders as the court, plus Arlene Armistead, who was a baton twirler. Shannon's attendant from my class was Caitlin Hardesty. I'd sort of known her in ninth grade. So that was the homecoming court. As Tanya said, "Let Shannon have her moment. Why not?"

It turned out too cold to go to the game, and we didn't know anybody who went to the dance, which was in the gym.

"Imagine getting dressed up for the *gym*," Tanya said.

Caitlin Hardesty went because she was in the court. Some junior took her. I didn't know who. You can't know everybody.

The semester picked up speed from there. With winter on the way we had our first trip into the city.

Tanya and Natalie and Makenzie and me. It was to see the Radio City Christmas show, just for a laugh. With all the Rockettes as toy soldiers and the bogus cannon that knocks them all down. And 3-D Santa Claus.

We went into town on an early Saturday train and shopped all morning. Then we left our packages at Tanya's aunt's and went across town to Radio City for the matinee. My mother gave me some grief about going. But I arranged to be with my dad in White Plains that weekend and went into the city from there. It was great.

━◁○▷━

THEN IT WAS the new year. The juniors were working up their committees for the prom they'd give the seniors in May. Makenzie didn't seem to notice. But Tanya gave her a little nudge. "Go for it, Makenzie," Tanya said. "Get on one of the committees by all means, *if you want to give it the time.*"

But Makenzie didn't. "Too American, the prom," she said. Which is what she always said about something she didn't want to do. Reminding us she was English.

We were into a new semester by now. Alyssa Stark had graduated early, midyear. Tanya said she would.

I didn't know if they'd e-mailed everybody with that picture of the pink baby. So I didn't know if that had anything to do with it. And Tanya didn't mention Alyssa anymore. It was like she had pushed DELETE, and Alyssa went into the trash.

Then it was sparkly winter, and Presidents' Day sales at the mall. Then it was spring with the campus carpeted in white and purple crocuses, and I still lived for lunch. Everything was fine. It was fun. Then it was over.

PART TWO
This Spring

· · · ◄O►· · ·

TANYA TEXTED ME, and I thought she must be in her Contemporary Crisis class because it was second period.

I was sitting there in the outdoor courtyard of school. I didn't go to second period these days. And in third period I saw my counselor. I could do pretty much anything I wanted to. People backed off and gave me all the room in the world. I could drift through the day. The endless day. I was in this separate space now, separate from everyone and even me.

Then Tanya texted.

> We're all 3 here at my aunt's in the
> city. Take the 3:50 train. Tell your mom
> you're at your dad's and vice versa.
> B there.

The sun glared on the screen, and the message melted. I hadn't been keeping my phone charged. But the important thing is that Tanya texted.

The bell went, and the courtyard filled up with classes changing. Not a big bunch. It was the Friday before prom, and a lot of people had manicure appointments.

It was warm now, way past crocuses, and people were looking ahead to summer. The guys were in Lacoste and long shorts, and the girls were less layered. Everybody back in flip-flops. Their quick glances bounced off me. I was back to being invisible these days. I wanted to be.

But I was there, more or less. On the bench with the phone in my lap, thinking about the first train into the city after seventh period. The crowd flowed on like I was gone already.

Then I remembered. Tanya was dead.

• • •—◄o►—• • •

CHAPTER FOUR

Third Period

ALMOST A MONTH ago on a Saturday afternoon without a cloud in the blue sky, my three best friends forever, Tanya and Natalie and Makenzie, were killed. Their SUV went off the Country Club Road and hit a tree. An apple tree in full bloom. Tanya was at the wheel, on her phone . . . with me.

I'd wanted to think my mother wouldn't let me go with them that afternoon, to the mall. But actually they hadn't asked me. They hadn't gotten around to it. Anyway, the whole trip was about prom dresses—that day they'd been planning since Halloween at least. The day they'd make their basic decision. Then Tanya would take Joanne back.

But then halfway to Nordstrom, Tanya called me. She started to. Just a few words: "Kerry, we're all—" Was she going to ask me to join them at Nordstrom? Or was she just monitoring me? She monitored a lot of people. She'd monitored Alyssa Stark to the day she graduated.

I thought maybe Tanya had hit the wrong button or dropped the phone or something. But in that moment the SUV must have been in the air. Over a ditch. And then the tree. They weren't wearing seat belts. They never did. We didn't. Remember Halloween? We were in and out of the car, so we didn't.

I tried to call Tanya right back, and got nothing. But by then they were gone, all of them. All the friends I had. Just like that. How can you exist in one moment and then *not* in the next? It wasn't real. None of it. It wasn't right, or what anybody wanted.

The school didn't have a grief counselor. Nothing as bad as grief was supposed to happen at a school like Pondfield. They had to bring one in. Then they held an all-school assembly to introduce her to us. It was like sophomore orientation in September, but for everybody. Then they got into a lot of talk about driver safety and seat belts and phoning from behind the steering wheel. Two phones went off during the assembly.

In that first week a lot of people got appointments with the grief counselor. It was a free period for a bunch of people. Shannon Grady and half her cheerleaders went. I pictured them there in the counseling wing, in uniform, doing one of their pyramids for our game against Ridgefield.

Sophomores went. It was like an orgy of grief before it was over. There were pictures on every phone of the car wreckage. The BMW wrapped around the apple tree, with the apple blossoms fallen on it like spring snow. Even pictures of the BMW after it had been towed.

That was the week of the memorial service, and the shrine. The shrine sort of happened against the apple tree. Loads of flowers and ribbons in school colors, blue and silver. Stuffed animals. Downloaded pictures of Tanya and Natalie and Makenzie, laminated to weatherproof them. A rosette of orange and black ribbon that must have been somebody's Halloween Hottie award. Somebody had left a vintage cell phone at the shrine. Which a few people said was in poor taste. But it just meant that Tanya died as she'd lived. She always networked and multitasked and kept her lines of communication open. She always had a finger on whatever was happening.

Anyway, Country Club Road wasn't particularly safe. There'd been talk about widening it.

But the flowers on the shrine were still fresh when people started scrambling. The senior girls did. Tanya and Natalie had been the top of the heap. Makenzie could have ruled the juniors if she'd felt like it. A ton of people wanted to be who they'd been, including some people nobody had especially noticed. Like Emma Bentley and Jocelyn What's-her-name. It wasn't going to work for them, but they scrambled.

And people moved on.

The seniors had heard from their colleges, so there was buzz and Twitter about that. Graduation too, coming up. And after that, summer and summer plans. Endless summer.

—◦—

AND NOW IT was May, the Friday of prom week. The prom posters were everywhere, and the juniors' committees were down to the wire. I personally thought they might call off the prom, out of respect. Nobody else seemed to think so. They had their dresses.

Nobody left *that* to the last minute. I was hearing a lot about dresses. You'd be surprised what you can hear when there's all this space around you.

I remembered last September and eating lunch alone and hearing every word from the conversation at the other end of the table. But back in September I hadn't known what alone was.

The other thing about this year's prom was that Tanya and Natalie had begun planning an after-prom party. *The* after-prom party. It was going to be—it would have been at Natalie's house, on the terrace and around the pool. Tanya didn't want the party at her house because of Joanne.

"She'd get off her StairMaster and be all over us," Tanya said. "She'd be everywhere we turned. She'd hack in."

So it was to have been at Natalie's, and they had ordered blue and silver T-shirts that read:

THE ONLY AFTER-PROM PARTY

They'd had forty of them silk-screened and handed out to let everybody know who was invited, and who wasn't.

The days moved on, and somebody put a couple of The Only After-Prom Party T-shirts on eBay. Now the buzz was all about the after-prom party at Chase Haverkamp's. And it was going to be given by guys. This was pretty outrageous because it was supposed to be girls who made the social rules. But what girl would dare? Emma Bentley? Jocelyn? Please.

So there was a lot of after-prom party buzz, which had zero to do with me.

The earth turned, but I didn't budge. I pretty much just logged off of life. There was still some hallway crying from various people. But I was probably the only one still seeing the grief counselor. I'd lost the most.

—◇—

SHE WAS ALL right, I suppose, as grief counselors go. She didn't tell me to turn my frown upside down or anything. She didn't try to patch me up with bumper sticker slogans. But needless to say, she wasn't helping. How could she? Something had been taken away from me that no adult could give back.

We'd had some bad sessions in that poky, windowless little cell of an office down at the end of the counseling wing. Every third meeting was with my parents, and they were the worst times. Even Dad didn't get it—

that you don't make new friends in high school. Not at Pondfield High School. You're lucky if you hang on to the ones you have.

"Honey, there must be plenty of kids who'd be glad to—"

But I had to cut him off. He didn't get it. It wasn't his fault, but he didn't get it.

Also, he couldn't see what an honor it had been. I was only this first-semester sophomore last fall when Tanya and Natalie and Makenzie took me in. Me. A nothing little tenth grader who knew zero about layering or labels or who was in charge. Even Dad didn't see the miracle of it.

My mother was way worse, of course. "Honey," she said, "Tanya and Natalie were seniors. They wouldn't have even been here next—"

"So you're saying they might as well be dead because they were going to graduate anyway?" I said, really screaming at her. Besides, Makenzie was a junior, and she'd have—

"I'm not saying that," my mother said. "But you can't blame me for being grateful you weren't in the car with them. And I think you need to use this time to—"

"Don't tell me to go out and get new friends!" I screamed. "Don't *you* start."

"I wasn't going to tell you that," my mother said. "I was going to say that maybe now you can begin to find out who you are."

Me? Who was I without them? My mother so didn't get it. My clueless mother. She couldn't see I was three-quarters dead myself.

⚊◦⚊

TODAY, THOUGH—NOW—everything was different.

I was smiling inside, grinning from ear to ear, all the way along the hall of the counseling wing. I'd turned my frown upside down because this big rock had rolled off me. Because Tanya had texted, and the nightmare was over, almost.

⚊◦⚊

THE GRIEF COUNSELOR was Ms. Gordon, but she'd asked me to call her Rosemary. I didn't want to, so I hadn't called her anything. She seemed to live and work out of an oversized tote bag with her other shoes in it. The only thing on her desk was a box of Kleenex.

I was braced for her when I heard voices coming out of her office. I'd forgotten this was a session with parents. They were there early, talking about me behind my back, which I didn't particularly like. I stopped outside the door because my mother was talking.

"I should have done something sooner," she was saying. "I should have nipped this in the bud. After that business last Halloween at the latest. Kerry was just too . . . grateful to be accepted. She was swept off her feet and didn't know which way was up. She didn't know what was real. These girls were too old for her. I was so busy playing hands-off suburban single parent and giving her all the freedom she—"

"Why are you overanalyzing this?" my dad said, breaking in. "You overanalyze everything. We're talking kids here. Kids. They're resilient. They move on. I never had a friend in high school I couldn't do without. All Kerry needs is time to—"

I walked in then. Dad was on one side, his chair tipped back, having his say. And looking at his watch. My mother was on the other side, as far from him as she could get. She was wearing her quilted Burberry and her concerned look.

I walked in, and I didn't need this now. I so totally didn't need any of this.

"I'm fine," I said to them in the old voice I hadn't used in weeks. "I'm done here."

Then I spun around and got out before anybody could say anything. Ms. Gordon could keep her Kleenex. I wasn't even numb now. I could feel my feet, slapping along the floor tiles. And where was my backpack? And my books? And what class did I have third period? Language Arts? Something. And what were we discussing in that class? *Lord of the Flies?* Whatever.

I was fine because Tanya had texted. And everything else had been a . . . mistake. A cosmic mistake. And I had to be on the 3:50 train into the city because in another miracle, Tanya had texted me.

I'd known all along this entire . . . situation had been too bad to be true.

—◄○►—

ONLY TWO OR three people got on at our station. I kept my head down. The train was mostly empty, running against rush hour. I wrestled out of my backpack and settled next to a window. The train jerked and rolled, and it dawned on me that at this particular moment in time nobody on earth knew where I was. The plastic seat sighed under me.

And in that exact second my phone rang. I froze. Why hadn't I shut it off? I didn't need anybody trying to stop me. I didn't even want another message from Tanya because I'd already had the one I wanted. Needed.

I rummaged in my backpack for the phone. It was my mother's number. I tapped her straight to voice mail. I'd already left her a message that I was going to Dad's up in White Plains. Which was enough. The White Plains train flashed past this one right now, loaded with commuters heading home.

From the corner of my eye I glimpsed my reflection in the window here on the shadowy side of the aisle. I sat shoulder to shoulder with myself. The two of me, the dead one I'd been and the live one now that Tanya had texted.

Tanya and Natalie and Makenzie. Their names sang in my heart and hip-hopped in my head. If only I'd known this morning that I was going to meet up with them, I'd have kicked myself up a little when I was getting dressed. Put forth a little effort on my hair. I wore it long and smooth, longer than shoulder-length, like Natalie's. But I hadn't done anything about it for days. I hadn't cared what I looked like for weeks. I'd have worn the same top two days running if I could have made it past my mother. I just didn't care. I kept to the dress code with a collar on my shirt. I tied a sweatshirt type top around my waist. I just didn't care.

The week after Easter there'd been a school day hot as June. One of those days when you can almost see the buds popping on the trees. Tanya had pulled her shirttails out of her waistband and tied them in a knot. You couldn't be sure if you were seeing her belly button or not.

She cut the dress code that close, and by lunch every girl in school had tied her shirttails in a knot and was showing skin. Every girl and three or four guys from the art department.

—◄○►—

THE TRAIN WAS braking for the Riverdale station already. My throat began to close up a little bit. The city was just ahead, tall and gray into the sky. I wanted to fast-forward and be there because doubts were creeping into my head. They nagged me like a mother.

What if that message Tanya texted was just . . . in my mind?

What if it was only something I wanted, not something that was?

Maybe when you're as lonely as I'd been, you hear

things and see things that aren't true. Maybe I was losing my—

No. That message was real. Totally. And nothing else was. That message had . . . punched the restart button and changed everything back to the way things were supposed to be.

The train lurched and rolled on, and just ahead across a river Manhattan rose. The windows at the tops of the high-rises burned with gold fire from the sinking sun.

125th Street then, and the plunge into the tunnel under Park Avenue. I could find my way around the city, more or less. As a family, when we'd been a family, we used to come in for *The Nutcracker* and ice-skating at Bryant Park and Dylan's Candy Bar at Sixtieth and Third. Only this past Christmastime Tanya and Natalie and Makenzie and I had come in for the Rockettes' holiday show. We'd changed clothes at the apartment where Tanya's aunt Lily lived. It wasn't that long ago. It was when things were real. I knew my way. I just didn't know what I'd find when I got there.

If anything.

The doubts nagged, and my heart pounded. We were coasting to a stop along the platform way down under Grand Central Station.

Just as I was struggling into my backpack, a guy stood up from his seat ahead. We'd meet at the door.

He was a blond-headed guy in Lacoste and long shorts, carrying a see-through garment bag with a blue blazer inside. I looked again, and it was Spence Myers.

Spence Myers with the triple 800s on his SATs and early admission to Georgetown. I clenched up like a fist. It was like I hadn't really escaped, or made a clean break. I panicked, but fought it.

I pulled me together. What did it matter? As a rule, you can see seniors, but they can't see you back.

"Kerry?"

We were meeting at the door, stepping out onto the platform. He was pulling the iPod out of his ear. I thought about my hair. The sweatshirt sagged around my waist.

"What are you doing in town?" said Spence Myers like we were old pals. He was editor of the school newspaper. Back at the beginning of the year I'd thought about going out for it, working on staff as a lowly sophomore gofer or something. But then when I got in with Tanya and Natalie and Makenzie, when would I have had the time? I needed to keep my time open. And in fact they were the only way Spence could know who I was. Because I was on the fringes of Tanya's group.

"I—I'm just coming in to have dinner with my dad," I said. "We're taking a late train back."

It was a Friday night. It made sense. Why shouldn't I be in town with my dad? I hadn't thought about needing an alibi. But here one was. It practically jumped out of my mouth.

"You?" I said, like we stopped for a chat in the school hall every day or so.

"Party tonight," he said. "Then I'm staying over for an interview in the morning," Spence said. "It's for a summer internship with a nonprofit. Then back for the prom tomorrow night, and the after-prom thing at Chase's. Big weekend."

Huge, I thought, almost losing the thread of why I was here. Why *was* I here?

"Who are you going to the prom with?" I asked him. It seemed a mature question. While in my head I could hear Tanya saying, *"Not Spence Myers. . . . He has some growing up to do. . . . I'll get back to him later."* I could hardly hear anything else.

"Bunch of the guys," he said, "keeping it real."

I didn't know where to go with this. He was a senior. He was all about internships and keeping it real and the prom with guys and early admission to—

"How are you doing?" Spence said to me as the gates got closer. "You still seeing the counselor?"

He knew that? I never thought people could see me unless I was with Tanya and Natalie and Makenzie. If then.

"Not anymore," I said. "Today was the last session."

"Ah. Well, it's good if you can move on," Spence said. "You have to."

He had. But then, had I ever seen him and Tanya together, just the two of them?

"It was all a mistake anyway," I said.

And he probably thought I meant seeing the counselor was a mistake. That's what he probably thought.

—◁○▷—

We were out in the station now, where National Guard soldiers patrolled in camouflage, with guns. People were everywhere, and sound bounced off the marble walls. Now we were crossing the concourse, this gigantic space with more people surging in every direction, swinging laptops, running for trains. Everybody moving from one world to another. And way up above all the stars of the galaxy, all the astrological signs, lit up against the turquoise blue ceiling.

I was a little numb again. It was all *Bright Lights, Big City*, and I was strolling through it with a major senior guy, so there was nothing particularly real about any of this.

"Your dad in Wall Street?" Spence asked.

"What?" My dad? Wall Street? My dad was in White Plains, miles from here, where he lived and worked. "Oh. Right. Yes, he works on Wall Street."

Lie Number Two, and Wall Street was downtown. Tanya's aunt's apartment was uptown. Two different directions. Two different trains. We were past the big clock and the newsstand now and almost at the subway entrance.

"You?"

"My folks have a place on Sixty-ninth," Spence said, "Lexington and Sixty-ninth. I'm staying there tonight."

That meant he'd be getting an uptown train. And I needed an uptown train too because Tanya's aunt lived on Seventy-second Street. But I'd just told him my dad was in Wall Street, or on Wall Street—however you say it. So I ought to be looking for a downtown train.

He was pulling a subway pass out of his pocket as we headed down another flight in a mob of people.

◄○►

My head whirled. I supposed I could take a downtown train. Then get off somewhere and switch over to an uptown one. But I could also get totally lost and end up living permanently in the New York subway system. Or Brooklyn. It was like a—I don't know what—like a bunch of mole holes. A maze. And the signs made no sense. None. You had to know what you were doing.

I'd be lucky to get on the right train, let alone get on the wrong train and then change to the right one. I had to get away from Spence. Here's how bizarre this whole business was—I was trying to dump one of the major senior guys in school. Also the best-looking. I was so off my turf I couldn't believe it. Also, I wasn't used to making my own decisions.

"You go ahead," I said. "I have to buy a ticket." He had a pass. He could just go through the turnstile and . . . vanish down the mole hole. This lower level was teeming with people. If enough people got between us, I could just melt away, delete myself.

"No, take your time," he said. "I'll wait with you till your train comes. It's a zoo down here, and there are weirdos."

He waited while I stood in the ticket line. I had this much time to think. And to wonder, in spite of my grief—would it have killed me to keep using lip gloss?

He was still there when I came back, dry-lipped, ticket in hand. "Actually," I said, "I'm meeting my dad uptown. He's having a drink with some people. At somebody's . . . apartment." *Lie Number*—

"Come on then," Spence said, and I followed his swaying garment bag through the turnstile. He had a college haircut already, the blond hair at the back just brushing his shirt collar. In fact he was an Abercrombie & Fitch ad, except he had his shirt on. Now we were elbowing our way down more crumbling steps to the number 6 uptown train.

On this platform the tricky part was to keep people from pushing you onto the tracks. Some of these women were armed with handbags the size of Hummers. A train was charging in, a number 6. The tracks lit up.

If enough of a crowd got between us, I could just dart into a different car. It was dawning on me that Spence and I were headed for the same subway stop,

Sixty-eighth Street–Hunter College. I began to edge away, but he slipped a hand under my elbow to keep us together. A perfect gentleman.

Then we were in the subway car, plastered against complete strangers. "What stop?" he mouthed through all the noise.

Why didn't I say the stop after Sixty-eighth Street–Hunter College? Why didn't I just stay on the train when he got off and then walk back or something? Because I didn't know the stop after Sixty-eighth Street–Hunter College.

"Sixty-eighth Street–Hun—"

"Me too." Spence nodded, and the train thundered on.

—◄○►—

We fought our way up out of the ground onto Lexington Avenue against a tidal wave of Hunter College students going the other way.

It was almost dark now up here on the street. "I'm fine," I said.

"Where you heading?"

"Seventy-second Street," I said. One of my rare true statements. But what direction should I—

"I'll walk you to—"

"No, it's okay," I said.

"Then I'll peel off at Sixty-ninth," Spence said. "My family's place is at One twenty-nine, up there on the corner." We were walking past the big stone castle part of Hunter College. "Didn't Tanya's aunt Lily live on Seventy-second?" he said.

". . . Somewhere around there," I said.

I guess I could have told him I was going to see her. Pay her a call. But Tanya's aunt Lily officially lived in Paris. She was a stylist, or had been. She wrote about fashion or something. She wasn't in New York that much, and Spence might have known. Who knew what people knew? Besides, I didn't want him walking me right up to her door. I couldn't chance it.

Tanya's aunt Lily had been there at the memorial service, from Paris. She must have been her great-aunt or something. She was an old lady, dressed all in black. A lot of people were that day, except hers was Paris black. She was the only woman at the service in a hat. With a big black brim.

Joanne had picked her up at JFK Airport and had taken her back there that night. I don't even know why I knew that, or remembered. I was missing whole blocks of time.

"You going to be cool?" Spence was saying to me. We were at the light at Sixty-ninth.

"I'm going to be fine," I said. "I'm practically there."

"If you're sure," he said. "See you at school."

I watched him cross Lexington Avenue, all the way up to the canopy of his building. Then I walked on toward Seventy-second Street and let the sidewalk crowds swallow me up.

That was the moment I was most alone. The sun was still bright on the windows of the penthouses, but it was evening on the street. When I turned into Seventy-second Street, I saw I'd have the doorman to deal with.

In movies New York doormen wear top hats and gold braid and open the doors of limos. In real life they wear parts of their uniforms and stand out by the curb, having an endless conversation with each other. With any luck I might just breeze into the door of Aunt Lily's building. Whisk right in.

The canopy was dead ahead. And what was I heading for? Anything? Nothing? In two minutes would I be walking back the way I'd come, from one emptiness to another?

Trees grew in pots beside the front door. The doorman was there, blocking the way. Just my luck. A young guy. The night shift? He looked me over.

"Miss Garland's apartment, please."

He reached inside the door for the receiver of an old-time intercom telephone. "I don't know if anybody's up there," he said. "But I'm part-time. And I just came on duty."

He was poking a little metal button. Somewhere high above us a bell was ringing in Aunt Lily's apartment. And echoing in my head.

And I thought, just for a moment: I'm on my own here. I can still back out. I can make this not happen.

"I'm her niece," I said, for some reason. *Lie Number Three* or so. "She's my aunt."

But then he said, into the intercom phone, "Young lady to see you."

I swallowed hard. I could feel my spine all the way down. The doorman jerked his head. "You can go on up."

Who? Who had said I could go on up?

I was crossing the dark-paneled lobby now, under the heavy beams. I was walking on eggs, not looking back for fear he'd change his mind. Forty-nine percent of me wanted to turn back. Run.

In the elevator I pushed 13, the button just below

PH for penthouse. So if it was Aunt Lily up there, or her maid, I needed to have something ready to say—ready and rehearsed—another alibi. Unless—

The elevator door rolled back, and I stepped out into a shadowy space. It wasn't very big, with Chinese wallpaper and dim lights behind parchment shades. Only a couple of doors because there were only two apartments on a floor, two huge and echoing apartments. I was turning to the door of Aunt Lily's when the door to the back apartment opened. The door cracked and then creaked, and someone was there, behind it in dark shadow.

I only caught a glimpse. It was someone ancient and weird with eerie orange hair. She was wearing dark glasses in this gloom. And an apron. I flinched, made myself look again, and the door was closed.

I turned then, to the other one. I didn't knock. I didn't have to. The door was inching open, and before I could see, a scent drifted out to me. The scent of apple blossom.

CHAPTER FIVE

Glitter City

IT WAS BRIGHTER inside. Light fell across the marble floor and washed over me. Not blinding, but I couldn't see at first. I couldn't focus.

I heard a little chortling, chuckling laugh or two, muffled behind hands. The laughter echoed out of some distant place. But they were right there, standing together in the mirrored entrance hall.

Tanya was.

Tanya with highlights in her blond hair and her hand on her hip and her eyebrows arched. I'd know her any-where. It wasn't a picture of her. Or a holograph or what-ever. Or a memory. Or something made out of mist. It was Tanya. The best-looking girl in school because she could make you think so.

And there beside her, Natalie—perfect Natalie. Actually the prettiest when you came right down to it. Natalie with the violet eyes and the natural darkness beneath them. And the double lashes. And on Tanya's other side—Makenzie, smiling her slightly sassy smile, with her arms crossed before her. Full of life, all three, and realer than anything that had happened to me for weeks. There they were, dressed for a Saturday at the mall.

I was hyperventilating, but Tanya cut right through that. She looked me up and down. "Flip-flops? In town? Honestly, Kerry. And what is that tied around your waist, something from American Apparel? And your *backpack?*"

"Honestly," Natalie echoed. "What next? Tank tops?" And Makenzie only smiled because she could probably remember being me.

Then all I could see was the crystal chandelier on the ceiling of Aunt Lily's entrance hall. My eyes swam, though I thought I'd cried all my tears.

Then all of us, all four, were swimming, drifting like seaweed in turquoise waters among the fish and crabs and rams of all the astrological signs, a zodiac sea mirrored like the walls of Aunt Lily's entrance hall. A mirrored sea, veined in gold, scattered with silver shells, and in every shell a pearl.

I woke up—came to on the white sofa in Aunt Lily's living room. It was a room out of a dream anyway, with murals on every wall, of French clowns—diamond shapes on their costumes and ribbons crisscrossing up their legs. And ladies in masks being helped out of gondolas in Venice. The landscape of a dream, and peeling a little with the years. A little out of date.

Every light was on. I struggled up among the sofa pillows and looked around. All the painted people on the walls were jostling each other like the subway crowds.

And *they* were still there, close enough to touch. Makenzie sat curled in a kidney-shaped love seat just her size. She'd always had somewhat rebellious hair—haystacky, and her glasses were propped up there where they always were.

Natalie sat in a French-looking chair with gold arms. Every little move she made was always worth watching. Her hands tucking her long black hair behind her ears was an event. Always had been. Tanya sat forward in another French chair.

"Kerry," she said. "Get a grip. You're scattered. And don't faint again. You drooled."

"What time is it?" I said.

That seemed to be good for a laugh. Makenzie chortled behind her hand. Natalie rolled her violet eyes.

"What does it matter?" Tanya asked.

It didn't, I supposed. But I never wear a watch, and I wondered. After all, I'd been out like a light, long enough for them to carry me in here. I'd felt their hands on me, even when I was out like a light. Their hands, making contact.

"Time doesn't matter, Kerry," Tanya said. "Let's get that straight. Stay right here in the moment with me. *Here* is what matters. Where's your phone? Don't tell us you didn't bring it."

I looked around for my backpack, and my head was splitting open.

"Makenzie, get it out of her bag." Tanya snapped her fingers.

Makenzie sprang off the love seat and went for wherever my backpack was. When she came back with my phone, Tanya took it and flipped it open.

"How old is this thing?" she said. "Honestly. It looks like that one somebody left at the shrine. And what did you pay for it? Thirty-nine ninety-five?"

But while she was trash-talking my loser phone, she was punching in a number she knew by heart.

She'd just texted me this morning, so where was her phone? It seemed an age ago, not that time mattered. "Where's yours?"

"Good question," Tanya said. "I think the contract got canceled. It figures. You were the last call, and now it's dead as a doornail. I threw it out. I'm good at getting rid of anything I can't use. But then we couldn't order in lunch. Aunt Lily canceled her landline because she's in Paris so much. She can be so uptight about money. You know old people."

"And as a matter of fact, we're starving," Natalie said. "I personally could never be anorexic. I don't know how Joanne does it."

"There's nothing in this entire apartment but Bloody Mary mix, cans of Slim-Fast," Tanya said, "and—"

"Cocktail olives," Makenzie said, "which we ate. We have to keep up our strength."

So now Tanya was on my phone, ordering.

"No anchovies on mine," I said as in a dream. "I hate anchovies."

"Anchovies?" Tanya stared. "Kerry, I'm not order-ing in pizza from, like, Yonkers. This is New York. I'm ordering actual food. Continental cuisine from Orsay on Lexington. They've been sending meals over to Aunt Lily for forever. I can put everything on her bill."

Oh, I thought.

"No snails," Makenzie was calling out. "No frogs or frog parts. I'm English."

My head had been pounding, splitting. Now it rang. All of this was happening. You could see it. You could hear every word. But how?

"Nothing with clams," Natalie was calling out. "You know about me and clams."

But the room was beginning to tilt and turn, and their voices wavered up from the bottom of a well somewhere. A deep, deep well. The costume people painted on the walls made jerky little moves. The prisms on all the lamps tinkled. All I had to do was close my eyes, and I was back at the memorial service, a memory that came and went and wasn't real. Like a black-and-white movie you don't want to rent.

—◀◯▶—

It had been held at school because they needed an auditorium that big. A Saturday right at the end of April. The stage was decorated in branching blossoms, sprays of dogwood and pear and quince and Japanese cherry. Everything but apple blossom.

The whole school came. Hundreds. Cars backed up

for blocks. SUVs parked in ditches. It didn't matter that it was Saturday. Everybody came. Tanya's dad and Joanne. Her aunt Lily in the big black hat. Natalie's parents. My parents, together with me between them—me, stoned on some medication the doctor prescribed. Three pills. I needed more. The school chorus sang "You'll Never Walk Alone." How wrong they were.

They weren't there. Not their . . . bodies. It wasn't a funeral. The funerals had been private or graveside or something. Makenzie had been cremated, and her parents had taken her ashes back to England. The Kemps weren't at the memorial. Probably a community-wide memorial service was too public for them. Too American.

I never saw their bodies. Never. You don't see dead bodies in Westchester County, except on TV. What made me so sure they were dead? Who did I think I was? I ought to get over myself. They'd always been above the law, those three. They'd made their own laws. Tanya had.

The school orchestra played "When You Walk Through a Storm, Hold Your Head Up High."

And that was probably a sign. They'd probably just gone for a walk.

◄❍►

I OPENED MY eyes, and everything was clearer than before. The room was brighter, and the colors stronger, even on the fading walls. Tanya and Natalie and Makenzie popped out of the scene, realer than before. I saw what they must have been up to.

They'd spent the afternoon making themselves up with Aunt Lily's cosmetics. I'd been in her bathroom at Christmastime, so I happened to know: She'd cornered the world market on paint, powder, moisturizer, liner, and blush. She had enough pore filler to grout this building. They were ready for their close-ups. They were on stage now, and this apartment was the perfect setting.

"Yes, that sounds fine," Tanya was saying. She could sound exactly like a grown woman on the phone. She was as adult as she needed to be. "Dinner for four, and you can surprise us with the dessert. And Miss Garland would like it as soon as possible. Her party is going out later."

Natalie drew in her cheeks at that, showing her killer cheekbones. Makenzie grinned. We were going out later? Really?

"And add the usual tips for yourselves and the deliveryman," Tanya said, very brisk, snapping my phone shut, not handing it back to me.

Time narrowed and widened. Then in no time at all the doorman was buzzing up the word that the dinners were here.

"Kerry, go to the door and bring it all in. Deal with that."

And of course I did.

◄○►

THE DIAMOND-PANED windows of Aunt Lily's long dining room looked out on the nighttime glitter city. The curtains were taffeta in faded pastels, swag over swag. Fringe. Tassels. Dust hung in the swing of the swags. The chandelier over the table was filmy with gossamer cobwebs. Nothing had changed in this place for years, decades. Time had stood still.

We dimmed the chandelier and dined by candlelight. We unfolded the damask dinner napkins and settled around the silvery table in this grown-up room for our grown-up dinner. The four of us, having another adventure, around the table again like on Halloween night. In business again in these pools of candle flame. They'd pulled up the drawbridge, and I was on their side of the moat.

Was I still being nagged by doubts? Not this minute. You didn't have doubts for long around Tanya because she was always so certain. Tanya never let doubts in the door.

We took turns being the maid, bringing in the courses from Aunt Lily's huge institutional kitchen. We all played maid except for Tanya, who sat at the head of the table in a high-backed chair with arms. What was she like, there on her throne? Like always—the Mistress of Whatever Was Happening. The Queen of Now.

Makenzie was the soup course, a cool soup with a floating island of cream. She brought it in on one of Aunt Lily's dented silver trays. Natalie was the main course. Mahimahi, a fish flown in from someplace where A-list fish live—some turquoise sea. The fish was on a bed of something with whipped squash in a shape and a spray of asparagus Hollandaise.

It was truly adult food, and some of it went over my head. Besides, I kept snatching glances at the others, just to prove they were there, I suppose.

Makenzie was tucking in with knife in one hand and fork in the other, the English way. Natalie picked delicately through the sauces in case of clams. I'd forget to eat for watching them. I had this history of watching them, trying to be them. Tanya had to tell me to go to the kitchen for the desserts.

A swinging door led to a long butler's pantry lined with endless glass-fronted cupboards. Then a vast kitchen opened up—an acre of black-and-white lino-leum and tiled walls and hanging on them blue-bladed knives of every size. A truly historic refrigerator up on legs. The lighting was ghastly, from fluorescent tubes.

And just as I walked into the glaring kitchen, some-body walked out of it.

I stopped dead. I couldn't scream, or budge.

Somebody had been in here, over by that door to a back hall. Someone had been right there. Just a flash, a glint of ceiling light off of glasses. An apron? Then nobody, not even footsteps.

I tried to pretend it hadn't happened. What was I supposed to do—grab a bread knife off the wall and light out down that hall, wherever it led? No way.

I found my breath and yanked the desserts out of their insulated bag. My hands were all over the place, but I was in a big rush now. The desserts were true art-works, spun sugar curlicues poking up out of chocolate-encrusted ice cream bonbons. Whatever. I slapped them on a tray and got out of there, heading for the dining table voices. And believe me, I didn't look back.

Later, after dinner, when we were loading the dishwasher, I made sure I wasn't by myself. We bustled around the kitchen before we went to get dressed. And I kept right in the middle of the bustle. But I didn't tell the others somebody had been there. I just didn't, for some reason. Now, maybe I wasn't that sure I'd even seen anything, or anyone. Maybe it wasn't anybody real. How many kinds of *real* are there?

CHAPTER SIX

Blue Velvet Night

THERE ARE CLOSETS. Then there are walk-in closets. Then
there are dressing rooms. Then there was Aunt Lily's
entire ecosystem for her clothes, makeup, jewelry, her
whole history. It was a vast windowless space the size
of Costco.

And it went all the way back to her ancient child-
hood. She'd grown up in this apartment. There were
drawers full of Raggedy Anns and roller skates and
Shirley Temple books.

But most of it was like forever Fashion Week,
crammed with discounts and freebies from the last
fifty years or so. And mirrors everywhere you looked.

There you were in every closet door. Parts of yourself.

"Check this out," Tanya said, throwing open a pair of doors. Inside were shoe racks to the ceiling, two hundred pairs of shoes, at least. Then that rack pulled out, and another rack behind it had two hundred more—every open-toed, slingback, platform, ankle-strap, wedgie, spectator style since 1950 or whenever.

"Look." Tanya pulled out wide drawers that unrolled themselves. Inside against plush black steps was Aunt Lily's jewelry, a treasure chest of retro-bling. The whole room flashed with emerald and sapphire and ruby lights. Natalie sighed. Makenzie stared. The earrings hung on earring trees, three hundred miniature chandeliers, at least.

"This is just the costume stuff," Tanya remarked. "She keeps the hard rocks in the bank. And the furs in storage. But look here."

Behind more doors were shelves full of bags, silk and paper with grosgrain ties in designer colors. They were the freebies you get at fashion shows, mostly Paris and Milan. And the main source of Aunt Lily's cosmetic supply. The mother lode.

"Look at all this stuff," Tanya said. "It's like . . . plunder." She handed me a swag bag from Chanel. Inside, it was all there: the square bottle of Chanel No. 5, a lace fan, a dried-out bottle of Ultra Correction Cream, a compact with the Chanel logo. Crumbly bath salts, an evening bag on a long silk cord. All of it from probably 1964.

"Aunt Lily is such a squirrel," Tanya said. "Will she ever need this stuff? Or use half of it up? Even she doesn't need this much pore filler." Tanya looked in a mirror at Natalie and Makenzie. "But she won't put it on eBay either. You don't just give everything up and . . . walk away, do you?" she said to them. "Do you? You hang on to your life."

There was silence then, echoing like a bell that hadn't rung. Time teetered and stood still again. Then Tanya was throwing open more doors, and racks of dresses slid out—burst forth. "Frocks," Makenzie called them. Their hangers were on motorized carousels that revolved in the room, making the turning dresses and skirts whisper and caress each other. They sighed to be worn.

How long did it take to see even a little of all this? Even a fraction? Aunt Lily was the goddess of the goodie bag and the give-away. Forget the scarf and handkerchief drawers. Never mind the glove stretchers and a bin full of squirmy objects labeled: "Playtex girdles."

But time didn't matter, and we had to see everything—check everything out and try on everything but the girdles. We had to go through everything before we could decide what to wear. We had to put together outfits that worked for us out of this landfill of vintage outrageousness. We were going out. We had to look good, and a little older than we were. Because getting dressed together is the best part of going out. "Like who doesn't know that?" as Tanya always said.

Hair, of course, was major. Makenzie's haystack with her glasses embedded in it had to be jelled into semi-spikes with a subtle swirl of color not from nature. Nothing pink, nothing punk. Just a nod in the direction of pastel punkery to go with Aunt Lily's wasp-waisted lace dress Makenzie wore over leg warmers. It was hard to get Makenzie out of her favorite fringed suede boots. But tonight below lace and leg warmers she wore spike-heeled pumps. Patent leather. She had to pad the toes with tissue paper because her feet were so tiny.

"I feel reasonably sure I won't be able to walk a step in these shoes," she remarked. "I should think I will sit down suddenly on the pavement and break my little—"

"Mirror here,
Mirror there,
Mirror, mirror everywhere,"

Natalie chanted, turning in the dressing space, seeing several thousand of herself merry-go-rounding around. She'd found shoes like Dorothy's ruby slippers, but with platforms. They turned and turned and pointed in every direction on the snow-white rug. Aunt Lily's underwear department was itself the size of Switzerland. Natalie had raided it for a totally crazed strapless black bra to wear under a 1950s off-the-shoulder red satin number. And long black satin gloves that reached up her arms, over her elbows. Her hair was perfect as it was. It was never not perfect, and blue-black in this light. She pinned a jewel or two in it, out of the plush drawer.

My hair was a toxic area. "You have so let yourself go lately, Kerry. Honestly, you look like you teach math," Tanya said, and everybody agreed, even me.

What my hair needed was blow-drying and styling and anything to give it some life, some light, some lift. They did what they could. They performed an intervention. I wanted mine exactly like Natalie's, absolutely as smooth as falling water. Though my hair wasn't blue-black. My hair never could decide what color it was.

We were all in the bathroom now, the one off the dressing area. Kind of a 1920s bathroom with a tub up on claw feet. They'd spent the afternoon, maybe longer, making themselves up. Now they started over. Tanya was working foundation or something into her face. "Botox and soon now," she said.

"So soon?" Natalie murmured behind her. "When?" This apartment was a house of mirrors, but we all four were bunched before this one, over the marble sink.

Botox? I barely knew what it was. Wasn't it needles full of stuff old ladies shoot into their foreheads to smooth out the lines? And into their withered old cheeks? Maybe even into their—

"And how would we pay for Botox?" Tanya was saying. "Stick it on Aunt Lily's bill? I don't think so. There are limits. I suppose you still don't have a credit card, Kerry? A debit card?"

I didn't, of course. Somehow I wasn't ready for a world of charge-it and Botox. I didn't know the difference between credit and debit. The only card in my backpack was a discount card from CVS Pharmacy. I was always a step behind. I *lived* back here.

"See right there?" Tanya was showing Natalie a place on her forehead. "I don't know if I can go another day." She'd already worked wrinkle cream over all her skin that showed, and pancake makeup.

Makenzie and Natalie both examined whatever was happening to Tanya's skin. She was showing a certain amount because she'd found a vintage black leotard with scoop neck. Over this she'd added two flouncy short skirts that clashed with each other perfectly. And patterned stockings with strappy shoes. It didn't matter what she wore. She was Tanya. You saw her first, whoever else was there.

Then they turned back to me, remembered me. "Kerry's the real problem," they agreed. "She's got to look eighteen at least, or we can't take her anywhere."

I had to be refitted from the skin out. Tanya had whipped the sweatshirt from around my waist, carried it away in two fingers, and dropped it somewhere.

I needed a look that said prom night now—that said

senior year and then some. Sequin sleeveless top over black skirt that clung, then flared. Heels so high I was practically as tall as Natalie and practically towering over Makenzie. The shoes came to perfect points at the toe. Real instruments of torture—black lizard with ribbons that wound up my black-stockinged legs.

Nothing about me said tenth grade. Nothing. Nothing.

It was basically all about bras, as Natalie said. She had gone all through the bra bin and come back with one that had an underwire. Now when I looked down my sequined self, it seemed to be somebody else. And I couldn't see my feet. And I didn't look bad for somebody who was in a retainer fifteen months ago. Not bad at all.

I wasn't the only one who needed a bra intervention. They'd had to talk Makenzie out of her sports bra. But they did, and now she and I both had bosoms that could take us anywhere. Hers weren't as spiky as her hair and heels, but they certainly made a couple of points. We looked at each other and screamed.

Where were we by then? Not the bathroom. No, we were in Aunt Lily's bedroom, her master suite on the other side of the dressing area. She had a bed in there like Cleopatra's barge, except it was king-size, not queen. Big, swagging curtains kept out the night. The old disconnected ivory telephone at her bedside had a rotary dial. A strong scent of Aunt Lily's perfume hung in the room, lily of the valley. There wasn't a mirror on any wall, and that was better. There'd been thousands of us in the mirrored dressing room. Now it was just us four. Taller in our heels, swirlier in our skirts, bigger and bustier in our bras. I was the only one who didn't need major makeup. Just a little something to make my eyes pop. Too much makeup too young is always a dead giveaway, Tanya always said. Too much makeup is always about being the most desperate girl in ninth grade.

Though as Tanya also said, "A little lip gloss wouldn't kill you, Kerry."

There we were in a room that had never changed, the four of us in a dangle of earrings, a wobble of heels, in a cloud of Arpège perfume out of a swag bag. The Arpège fought a little with the lily of the valley, and just under that, apple blossom.

Jewels smoldered in Natalie's hair. Tanya's was simple and brushed back in that usual way of hers that could find all the lights in the room. Everything she did worked. Makenzie in glitter eyeliner was a whole different breed of Makenzie. Our skirts murmured against each other, urging us on. I suppose that was the moment when I was happiest.

But I wondered. Were we really going out? Not that we needed to. We were our own music and the audience for each other.

"How can you?" I dared to say.

And they totally knew what I meant. How could they go out when everybody thought they were—

"It's New York, Kerry. It's not Pondfield Podunk High School." Tanya's new eyebrows arched to the moon. "Kerry, it's the world. Try really hard to keep up."

And now we were going, this minute. We'd slung the long cords of our little purses over our stunning shoulders. Tanya's was a silver clutch. And we were staggering for the front door in our heels.

The long hall to the front entry was a gallery of giant framed blowups of fashion models from some other time. It was the decade when models had only one name: Carmen. Dovima. All in plain little black dresses and white gloves like Jackie Kennedy or Audrey Hepburn. Dead ladies, and gorgeous, larger than life in full black-and-white.

Except for the last poster. It wasn't from a fashion shoot. It was for a Hollywood movie, in full color and then some. A Hollywood movie star with flame-colored hair in a movie with purple mountains in it. Blazing red hair, purple mountains, Kelly-green satin dress. "RHONDA RANDOLPH," the poster proclaimed, "NOW IN VISTAVISION." She was in a dress cut down to here. She was practically spilling out of the frame.

You couldn't just walk past her. She could have stopped traffic.

"That's Aunt Lily's neighbor," Tanya said. "Rhonda Randolph. At least she used to be. She doesn't look anything like that now. Except for the hair."

"I saw her when I came in," I said.

Tanya turned that gaze of hers on me. "You rang the wrong bell?"

"No. She was at the door to the back apartment when I got off the elevator. She was watching."

Makenzie and Natalie looked at Tanya. "Oh, that would have been her maid, Flossie."

"She had that red hair," I said.

"Flossie wears all of Rhonda Randolph's stuff, even her wigs," Tanya said. "It couldn't have been Rhonda. She can't get out of bed. She's on, like, life support with oxygen tanks. She has to be ninety-five." Then we were in the entry hall, multiplied by the mirrored walls, under the tinkling crystals.

"Did you say anything to her?" Tanya asked me. "The maid?"

"No. She was just there. Then she was gone."

Tanya was looking out of the little peephole in the front door before she opened it. But there was nobody out there, nobody we saw.

We filled up the elevator, and our skirts overlapped. We dropped through all the lighted floor numbers, and now a thought nagged me. A question. When we got down to the lobby and the world, might it be just me, alone when the doors parted? After all, who else had seen them but me? I'd been the one sent to the door to deal with the deliveryman when our dinner came.

"How much money do you have?" Tanya said behind me, into my rhinestoned ear.

I had something like two twenties and a bunch of ones and my return train ticket to . . . wherever.

They all sighed. "We better walk," Tanya said.

"Will it cost to get in?" Makenzie wondered.

"Not for us," Tanya said. "But not everybody gets in."

"How will we?" Makenzie asked.

"Because I always get what I want," Tanya said, and the doors opened.

We four were chattering and clattering across the lobby now. And I was not alone. I was so not alone. We were there, all of us, making unnecessary noise. It was a spring night outside. It ought to have been five in the morning, but it wasn't. Seventy-second Street was bumper-to-bumper with limos and buses. The door-men were all out by the curb, talking to each other in no known language, cupping cigarettes in their hands. Another shift, the graveyard shift. I didn't see the young guy who'd let me in.

Then we were on the corner of Third Avenue by that river of yellow cabs flowing north in the city that never sleeps. While we waited for the light, Tanya explained about the place we were going. It was called Fabian's, the hot spot of the season. The place with all the vibe and the right mix of uptown and downtown, of private school, art school, FIT, and funk. And not too fussy about checking girls' IDs.

Getting past the guards on the door, the bouncer guys, was all about confidence and the right look. And timing.

"Have you been there before?" Makenzie asked Tanya.

"No, but I read 'Page Six' online in *The Post*," Tanya said. "What else is there to do in Contemporary Crisis?"

Then somehow we were there. Second Avenue? Around there, a darker avenue in the petal-soft night. A line of people stretched down to the corner, waiting to get in—on their phones, checking themselves out, hoping to make the cut.

Tanya was striding past them, up to the dim door of Fabian's. She glowed in the night, and her heels rang on the sidewalk. She glanced back, and her gaze gathered us up. Then she reached around the others for me. She took my hand and held it, made that contact. I supposed it was because I was the youngest. The guy at the door, huge in a muscle shirt with tattoos on his neck, was saying, "Well, well, what have we here?" So yes, he could definitely see them. He sure saw Tanya. I was so not standing there by myself.

The next thing I knew, we were just inside the door. Another muscle guy was doing a quick bag check and pat-down. It was all darkness and pulsing sound in here and a curtain to part. "Remember," Tanya said, letting me go, leading the way, "we're only here to try out the outfits to see if they really work. We're test-driving these dresses. They need to say 'Queens of the Prom and Then Some.' Otherwise, none of this is any big deal. Stay cool, don't drool. Look like you live it."

So, *Look like you live it* became our motto as the curtain parted and we were in a huge cube like a big blue velvet jewel box with stars on the ceiling. It was a big box throbbing with music and seething with people. Cube after cube, with glass stairways from one level to another, and more people than the subway. Pale preppies and downtown divas and the bridge-and-tunnel crowd—everything. And a certain amount of facial hardware. Everybody working overtime at being eighteen at least.

The DJ was famous, sitting up in a big neon box hanging in space. The bar ran for a block, with spotlighted bartenders. This must be what *vibe* means—the sound pounding your feet, the hands pointing at the ceiling, the snapping credit cards, the drinks in all colors. And how sure everybody was.

We were holding glasses now. We hadn't bought drinks. Who knew what they cost? We'd just picked up empties that people had left around. "Don't touch them with your lips," Natalie hissed. "You don't know where they've been."

How long were we there? Oh, I don't know. I don't know. It was wall-to-wall people, and the floor danced under us, and the guys circled. We moved together and apart. Then when we were on the glass stairs, lighted from below, it was the catwalk from Fashion Week or something. Or Paris. Yes, our outfits were working. They were so working. We were layered and lovely and looked like we lived it.

Makenzie's glitter lids sank in a sea of strangers. There was nothing left of her but the swirly spikes of her hair. Then a little later I found her again. Unknown hands had set her up on a bar. Now she was all crossed legs and leg warmers and spike heels. She seemed to be leading a sudden sing-along with a bunch of people— guys. I couldn't hear the song.

Later, I was leaning over a glass railing, looking down on a revolving dance floor. Tanya and Natalie were dancing down there in a space the crowds had cleared for them. Dancing together and apart. There was some strobe lighting, working with the turn of Tanya's mismatching skirts, Natalie's red satin. And the hair, always her hair tossing blue-black in the blue velvet room, and the black-gloved hands in the artificial air. Oh it all so worked. Guys circled, not knowing what move to make. Not so sure now.

Then I was on my own, drifting, looking for a restroom. Up one glowing staircase, down another. Along a row of private rooms now, VIP rooms in a hall with walls carpeted to muffle the noise.

I was by myself, but not long enough for doubts. Somebody walked out of a room and nearly ran me down. I was none too steady on these heels. It was this guy in a blue blazer, blond even in the dimness.

It was Spence Myers. Spence. Again.

We might as well be back at Pondfield Podunk High School. We were everywhere we turned.

He looked me over before he knew me. We were almost in each other's arms. "Sorry." He stepped back. "Kerry? That's not you, is it? *Is* it?"

I'd parked the wineglass somewhere by then, so I put out my hands, presenting me. All my sequins winked at him. My skirt sizzled. I didn't know if he could see the shoes, but I was definitely taller. And would you look at the figure? He wasn't sure it was me. Neither was I.

He grinned. "They say everybody turns up at this place. Though I'm guessing your dad's not here."

"No," I said. "Dad . . . couldn't make it."

"It really is you, isn't it?" He couldn't get over me. I'd so lost the backpack and the sweatshirt around the waist. I felt my head give a little move, a toss, the way Natalie worked her hair.

"I changed," I said, and he probably thought I meant the clothes.

It was just the two of us for a moment. Then it was over.

"I've been to a party." He nodded at the door he'd come out of, the VIP door. "It's the cast party for *Family Divided*. It opened tonight at the Broadhurst Theater."

I didn't know about plays on Broadway. Tanya would. She probably read the reviews online, during Contemporary Crisis, after she read "Page Six."

"A friend in the cast invited me to the party," Spence was saying. "Here she is now." He put out a hand to a girl coming out of the party room.

Did I know her? She was tall, dark hair, a little older, not really dressed for Fabian's. She'd just been on a stage. In a play. Was she a star? Did I know her?

"Alyssa, this is Kerry Williamson," Spence said. "Kerry, this is Alyssa Stark."

The world wobbled. The cat had my tongue. I remembered her picture on the living room wall of her house. Halloween. I remembered her bedroom and the jumble of things on top of the chest of drawers.

But I surely didn't look like anybody she'd ever seen before, even if she—

"You remember Kerry," Spence said, prompting her.

"Oh yes," she said. "I think our mothers know each other."

And what was that supposed to mean? I almost looked at her. I tried. "I was wondering where the restroom is," I said.

"Me too," Alyssa said. "Let's go together. It's better to go in pairs in a place like this."

A lot was going on in the restroom, and some of it could have been drugs. There was some money moving back and forth.

"They don't call it the powder room for nothing," Alyssa muttered in my ear.

When we got a stall, she stood guard for me. Then I stood guard for her. It was smoky chaos around the mirrors, which doubled everything and everybody. Downtown divas and Chapin girls. Dalton and Performing Arts. Everybody working over their faces, their hair, at the top of their lungs. And some of those tattoos were here to stay.

"This room is so New York," Alyssa said when we were at the sinks, "deafening, dirty, falling apart, jammed, nothing to breathe, and bring your own toilet paper. I love it."

She didn't have anything on her face. She must have washed off her theater makeup. Her voice was probably excellent for the stage—low, but you could hear, even in this place.

"How do you happen to be here?" she asked me.

"I'm with a bunch of people," I said—fast. "What's it like to be in a play on Broadway?"

"For me?" Alyssa said. "Actually, it's a lot like the first day of high school. You're the youngest, the newest, and everybody knows everybody but you. It's another language. And great. It's starting over."

"And that's a good thing?" I said.

"The best. High school goes on too long. Anything's better. But you need a plan. Mine was to get a walk-on part as somebody's daughter. I've got a lot to learn. If the play closes before fall, I'll enroll in the theater program at NYU. Thanks to your mother."

What? What did she say? My mother again? "My mother?"

"She's helping me with my application. And my backup. We e-mail a lot."

The world was wobbling so much that I may have gripped the sink.

"It's what she does, you know." Alyssa was studying me in the mirror. "College counseling and placement, helping with people's applications? Advising about the essays? Freelance?"

I nodded. I knew that. In a way, if I ever listened or noticed. That's what all those college catalogs coming in our mail were about. It's what my mother did on the computer all day in the room off our kitchen. It's how she made a living. Our living. I knew that.

But I was sinking fast. Sinking at the sink. Alyssa was saying, "I auditioned for the part in October. Took a couple of days off school for that."

In the mirror she found my eyes. I was working my hands with more stringy soap out of the dispenser—working and working and trying to think.

"And I got the part," she said. "To celebrate, Spence and I came into the city, to the Village and the parade Halloween night."

Halloween night. Yes, Tanya had known Alyssa was in the city that night, while I was—

"Then I graduated early so I could go into rehearsal."

What was Alyssa saying? That she'd been out of
school two days to audition? That she'd graduated early to
rehearse? Was she telling me there never had been a—

"And you know what, Kerry?"

We were talking too long at the sink. People were
pushing in behind us. Pushy people with elbows. We
ought to get go—

"The funny thing is that Spence Myers and I are just
friends. Tanya didn't have to worry about me after all.
I wasn't standing in her way. The only person standing
between Tanya and Spence was Spence."

I could feel myself going paler and paler. I wouldn't
look me in the eye in the mirror, or Alyssa.

"You know what her worst problem was?" Alyssa
said. "Tanya never knew what friendship was. She died
not knowing."

Now I was pale as . . . death. I'd looked past Alyssa,
and there in the jammed restroom door Tanya stood.
And coming in behind her was Natalie. And probably
behind them Makenzie. All Alyssa had to do was turn
and look, to follow my gaze. I couldn't have stopped her
or distracted her or anything. I was totally locked down.
All Alyssa had to do was see across that distance, ten or
twelve feet of filthy floor.

But she'd need to look fast—right now. Because Tanya saw us. She saw me there at the sinks in the hard light and Alyssa with me. Through all the crowds she saw us.

Tanya spun around. She pushed the others back. Their skirts furled. Natalie's hair swirled. And they were gone like they'd never been there to begin with.

CHAPTER SEVEN

Makenzie's Kilt

I GOT AWAY from Alyssa as soon as I could. I more or less ran for my life. They'd seen Alyssa. What if they saw Spence? What if Spence stepped out of that party room again, this time into Tanya's arms? I didn't know what that would mean. How could I?

My head felt terrible, like I really had been drinking. All I could think about was finding them, and getting away. There were too many worlds here, and they were getting all mixed up. My head was.

Now I was out in one of the giant blue cube rooms, under the sequin stars. I elbowed my way through to that staircase again, to look down on the packed dance floor. But they weren't there.

I looked everywhere, on every level, in the little alcoves where couples sprawled in black leather banquettes. I looked high and low and along the bar. A big hand with hairy knuckles and a class ring came out of nowhere and closed over my arm, but I twisted out of its grasp and kept moving, as fast as I could. When the panic began to take charge of me, I started looking for real air to breathe. Then I couldn't find that curtain in front of the door. Then I could, and I was outside, past the bag check and that bruiser with the tattooed neck.

It was still dark out here. It ought to be broad daylight by now, but it wasn't. People were still lined up, waiting to get in, taking pictures of each other with their phones, drinking things out of sacks.

And I was out here, gasping for breath, holding on to a parking meter. Then it hit me hard. They'd left me.

What did that feel like? It was just like Halloween night in Alyssa's bedroom with her mother blocking the only door. That moment when I heard Natalie's car start up and drive away over the mashed leaves. I was being left behind again. Dumped.

But it wasn't the same at all. It was totally different. And I wasn't in Alyssa's bedroom. Far from it. I was standing all by myself on a sidewalk in New York City, dressed to kill. And I could be.

Here came the panic again, and I was ready to run into the street. But I didn't. It wouldn't take much to break the heel off one of these ridiculous shoes. Then where would I be?

A cab or two went past, down Second Avenue, and I thought—take a cab. It can't be that far. It can't cost that much. I pulled the bag off my arm and unzipped it and poked around in it. But of course my money was in my backpack, at Aunt Lily's.

So I just began to walk back the way we'd come, along the line of people hoping to get into Fabian's. It was colder now, a lot. A sharp night breeze blew straight through my sequins, and my arms were bare.

On Seventy-second Street dog walkers were out and people were carrying newspapers out of the deli. I practiced regular breathing and not looking anybody in the eye. I so looked like a girl who'd just left Fabian's by herself.

Look like you live it, I heard in my head. And Spence saying, *That's not you, is it? Is it?* And Alyssa saying, *High school goes on too long.* And what had Tanya said? *You don't just give everything up and walk away, do you?*

Do you? You hang on to your life. Mirror here, mirror there, Natalie chanted in my head. *Mirror, mirror everywhere.*

My feet were killing me. I couldn't remember when I'd sat down last, except in the restroom stall. I could hear Makenzie in my head, clearly—

I feel reasonably sure I won't be able to walk a step in these shoes.

I had to sit down a minute, anywhere. The shoes were cutting my feet in four separate places. Right there an iron gate opened onto a postage-stamp garden, and steps up to somebody's front door. A stoop. I turned in and sat down on the bottom step and tucked my skirt. I sank into a pool of darkness. The next people walking past didn't even notice me there. Invisible again.

There were still all these voices in my head, and I couldn't untangle them. *Shut up,* I thought. *Shut up. Shut up.* I had to figure this out on my own. I had to get to what was real and decide what I needed to do. But I was no good at deciding things. And terrible at being alone.

I wanted to go home. It was Halloween night again, and I was drifting in the dark, trying to get to Linden Street. Or to Dad's in White Plains. I was out in the dark on my own again. For somebody who'd do anything to belong, why did I keep ending up alone?

And one more thing just like Halloween night: I didn't have any money.

The step, the stoop was freezing. I had to go back to Aunt Lily's. Of course they were there. Did I expect them to wait around till I got away from Alyssa? What if they ran into Spence like I did? Of course they left. They hightailed it out of there. I ought to get over myself.

I had to go back to Aunt Lily's for my backpack and my money and the train ticket and my normal clothes. How could I go home looking like some little . . . club bunny? Some little wannabe. And how far could I get in these heels?

It was only another long block and a half to Aunt Lily's canopy. No doorman at this hour, and the front doors were locked tight. I rang the bell. While I waited, I looked out under the canopy to see if there was any light in the sky yet. Any daylight over there in the east. But the night was still dark blue velvet.

I must have known then.

There wasn't any dawn yet, but surely something was dawning on me. Something had happened to time, something to do with Tanya. She could tamper with time. It was one of her talents. It always had been, even before . . . the apple tree.

She could make moments—whole hours—stand still. She used to do it at lunch all the time. And those hours we'd spent at Aunt Lily's, over dinner, then trying on all those clothes, right up to the moment we came down in the elevator. Hours and hours. Then at Fabian's we'd been there ages before I ran into Spence. This was time Tanya had stolen. It had to do with the hold she had on you. It had to do with always getting what she wanted. And we'd helped her. We went right along, living in the moment, her moment. I did.

Now I knew that much. But it wasn't much. It wasn't enough. I rang and rang the bell. Finally the night man came out of wherever he was. He was mostly unbuttoned, with a newspaper in his hand. This morning's paper? Last night's? He unlocked the door.

"I'm—"

"Go on up," he said, and I was in.

Halfway up in the elevator I wished I'd asked him if Miss Garland's . . . other nieces were already home. Maybe that's why he'd let me in without a hassle.

The elevator opened on thirteen.

And history repeated. Everything had been going in a circle all along. The door to the back apartment, the old movie star's apartment, was cracked open again. Again somebody was standing there, just inside in the shadow. That flash of fiery red hair, or fiery red wig. A faded-out apron. No face. The door closed too soon.

I whirled around to the other one, Aunt Lily's door. It too was open a crack, and on it a Post-it note, stuck at eye level where I couldn't miss it—

> Kerry,
> We're in the penthouse.
> Come straight up, one floor.
> TTKU
> Tanya

TTKU? Oh. Try to keep up.

But the front door to Aunt Lily's apartment was open. I could go in and change and get my backpack. I could decide for myself what to do before I went up to the penthouse. Or not. This was my time. I was getting so tired in this night that wouldn't end. But this was my time.

I pushed inside, under the crystal chandelier, and

there were too many of me in all the mirrored walls. It was like a mirrored birdcage in here. Too many million winking sequins and all my bare arms, goose pimply from the night air. The rhinestones in my ears were all the stars on Fabian's ceiling. And all the little purses on all my arms. Empty. Every one of them.

Something about this space was a warning not to go any farther. But I didn't hear that. I leaned back against the door, and heard it click shut. I wandered into the big living room. The only light came from the entrance hall, but there were the people on the walls, the French clowns and the masked ladies, almost moving. I walked on, around things, through doors. I never learned the layout of that apartment. There was always another hall, another door. Who knew where that back hall off the kitchen went? Then I was in the hallway with the poster women, Rhonda Randolph in Technicolor and Dovima and Carmen and all the others, dimmer and dimmer down the hall.

A light came from the other end, and that must be Lily Garland's bedroom. A faint lily of the valley scent hung in the air. Had we left the light on in there?

Yes, it was her bedroom with the Cleopatra barge bed and the heavy curtains that were probably still blocking out the night. We'd thrown only a few things around in this room. We'd done our major trying on and dressing in—

Somebody was right there. In the door to the dressing room. A figure stood there in the low light. I was barely inside the bedroom, and there she was at the other doorway. This was worse than that moment in the kitchen. Way worse.

She had me cut off from escape. No, she didn't. I was standing in the door to the rest of the apartment. I'd cut her off.

And she was holding my backpack.

Could it be Rhonda Randolph's maid? But I'd just seen her shut her front door. She couldn't be here now. Could she? And this woman didn't have red hair. At least not at the moment. Her hair was white and sparse. Flyaway hair. She stood there in a long plain robe with a fringed sash tied around her waist. And she wore glasses with tortoiseshell frames on a chain. She was like any scary old woman, except for the designer glasses. Tall and thin and wrinkled and colorless. Witchy. No makeup.

And she was holding my backpack.

"Who are you?" she said.

I was doomed. Doomed. Doomed. I kept turning up in the wrong house where I wasn't supposed to be. Then I got caught by women in bathrobes. I would have thought how unfair this is if I hadn't been more scared than I'd ever—

"I said, who are you?" Her glasses flashed. Otherwise I might have seen something in her eyes. I felt it anyway. Fear. I wasn't the only one. She took a step back. Her skirts stirred.

"Kerry Williamson," I said as history kept repeating, word for word. I came close to telling her I was Miss Garland's niece. I came *this close.*

"This is yours, then." She meant the backpack in her old, papery hands. I was still too scared to think straight. I could hardly hear her for the pounding of my heart under the underwire. But maybe I had as much right to be here as she did. She'd been through my backpack. I'd almost caught her at it. She'd seen the copy of *Lord of the Flies* and my name on the CVS card—all my stuff, my comb and—

"You weren't in the car," she said. It wasn't quite a question, and I knew the car she meant, the BMW. Tanya's SUV.

No, I wasn't one of them. And never had been. But I

was blocking the door, and she looked like she wanted to make a run for it.

"How do you come to be here?" she said in an old, tired voice.

"Tanya texted me," I murmured. I'd been eighteen all evening. Now I was fifteen again.

"How could that be?" the old woman said. "How could she do that?"

"The contract on her phone hadn't been canceled yet," I said, in a smaller voice still.

There was a sound now above us, something like rolling thunder. A sound of thunder coming in waves, far off.

"Listen," the old woman said. She dropped my backpack and pointed to the ceiling with an immensely long finger. I remembered all the fingers pointing to the ceiling and the stars at Fabian's, all the young fingers.

"What is it?" I asked in a whisper.

"Them," she said. "The three of them. Roller-skating. We used to skate up there years and years ago when I was a girl. My girlfriends and I. Jackie. Lee."

Did she meant that Tanya and Natalie and Makenzie were upstairs in the penthouse . . . roller-skating? I remembered that day when I came to school all upset after they'd left me behind in Alyssa's house, and they were wearing pajamas. Pajamas. I remembered that for some reason.

"Go now." The old woman's hands jittered. "Here, take your backpack and go. We'll be all right as long as we can hear them skating. Use the time before it runs out. Call your family and go."

"I don't know where my phone is," I said. I could feel her panic, cold on my face. There was enough for both of us. She looked over at the old ivory rotary dial phone by the bed, which was dead.

"Just go then. Straight home."

"Not like this," I said. "I need my own clothes."

She blinked at my sequins. She probably hadn't even noticed what I was wearing. "There's no time to change. You don't have that kind of time. Grab your things and stick them in your backpack."

"They're in there." Meaning the dressing room. I still wanted to keep my distance. I was still scared of her. I didn't know what was real.

She moved aside. "Hurry." Her voice was like leaves blowing along a gutter. Dry, dry leaves. "Hurry."

I had to pick through everything we'd left on the

floor. All the things we'd rejected, the not-quite-rights and the wrong sizes. You could hear the far-off thunder in here too. I found my flip-flops, and then my school skirt and top. I decided to forget my old underwear. Some crazy voice babbling inside me, some crazy person wanted to keep the underwire bra.

It was brighter in here, dazzling, and there were all the mirrors. Next to my sweatshirt Makenzie's skirt was in a wad on the floor, a little kilt-style skirt with a buckle.

I'd just noticed it when the old woman pointed down past me. She was standing over me, between me and the thunder. She'd been in such a panic to rush me out of here. Now she said, "Pick it up."

I obeyed her. I picked up Makenzie's kilt.

"Smell it," she whispered.

I held it up to my face, the handful of tartan wool. It smelled like it had been in a fire. It smelled of burning, but not leaves in a gutter. Worse than that. Way worse. It cut my eyes. It was awful, and I dropped it.

"Go right now," the old woman said in my ear. And I went.

I couldn't run. In these heels? But I made tracks, and she followed me, all the way up the poster hallway. We were in the glaring front entrance now, lots of us. She reached past me and got the front door open.

Then we were out in the shadowy hallway with the Chinese wallpaper and the shaded lights. Again, she reached past me to hit the elevator bell with a long finger. We were this close.

"Do you know who I am?" I felt her breath on my face.

"No," I said. "Are you the old movie star's maid?"

And at this exact second, the door to the back apartment opened, more than a crack. Standing there was the old movie star's maid, in the faded apron and the flame-colored wig. She gestured to the old woman to come into the back apartment. Quick.

But the woman's hand had closed over my wrist. I'd been afraid all along she'd do something like this—hold me back or something. Grab me. Where was the elevator? But she had something else to say, one last thing.

"I have lived a long time," she said. "And I am very near the end. But I have never known anything like this before, never seen anything like this."

The elevator opened, and it was brighter inside. She let go of me. "Run for your life," she said, and I lunged into the elevator.

As the doors closed, I saw her move toward the back apartment and the maid standing there. Flossie. I saw Flossie reach for her and pull her inside. Two panicked old women. You could smell their fear. The door banged shut, and the locks turned.

The elevator doors closed. And my hand came out to touch a button. It pushed PENTHOUSE.

CHAPTER EIGHT

Rolling Thunder

"COME STRAIGHT UP, one floor," Tanya's note had said, and so I did. It was either that or go wandering out there in the dark, finding my own way home. Alone again—the black, blank streets, the mole hole subway. Another Saturday without them. Anyway, I could feel Tanya from here, the tug of Tanya.

The old woman had said, "Run for your life." And, really, wasn't I? What kind of life did I have without them?

━◀◉▶━

THE ELEVATOR DOOR opened, and I was already in the penthouse. It seemed to be one gigantic apartment—the whole top of the building. You could have a party just here in the entrance hall. You could invite half the Fabian's people home and have a huge party.

But only one light was on, a naked bulb on a wall. No mirrors. Only faded squares where pictures had hung, or mirrors. The penthouse was vacant. I could feel the weight of room after room of emptiness where any little thing would echo and nobody lived.

I followed the thunder through a doorway with columns into another monster-sized room. The city lights flickered across the dust-curled floor through long windows. The penthouse seemed to be hanging in space— somewhere between the moon and New York City. I'd walked the whole length of the room, and I was standing in front of double doors now, with all that thunder just on the other side.

I waited with my hand touching the place where the doors met. I gave myself one last chance.

Then I pushed both doors open. It was a ballroom that looked onto a terrace and the night.

You couldn't believe a room this big in a New York apartment. Like an airplane hangar with an acre of parquet floor. And nothing in it but a few rickety little chairs along the walls where there must have been hundreds once. Once upon a time.

No lights on at all. Three giant chandeliers hung down, but they'd been tied up in big cloth bags. The only light came through the long French doors. It was beginning to be daylight, finally. But I didn't have time to think about that. I didn't have that kind of time.

Because here they came, the three of them roaring around the room on roller skates. They saw me and screamed, and the screams bounced and bounced off the walls and echoed across the ripply floor. They were speed-skating right at me, gripping each other, touching the floor for balance, practically falling but never quite. When had any of us been roller-skating?

But they were. Here they came in their Fabian's prom outfits. Tanya's billowing skirts. Natalie's peekaboo black bra and red satin dress. Makenzie in lace and leg warmers. But now, of course, they'd lost their stilty, strappy, stiletto heels and were wearing skates. Old-fashioned, lace-up skates. Dirty white leather.

It was great—fabulous. Tanya looked the most like a skater in her leotard under the skirts. But they were gray in this light. Even Natalie's dress was grayish. I dropped my backpack, and they were practically running me down, dragging toes to stop, throwing sparks. They had their ways of stopping. Makenzie tripped on my backpack. They were all totally out of breath. Their hands came out for me to steady them. I felt their hands all over my bare arms, and their warmth.

"Where have you *been?*" Tanya said, squeezing my hand. They all wondered. "You've been, like, ages. Eons. Lifetimes."

"I looked for you there," I said, trying to explain. "I looked all over and along the whole bar before I—"

"Whatever. You're here now." They were catching their breath. Tanya had already caught hers. "And honestly, what are you doing in those ridiculous shoes? Get out of them. Makenzie, go find Kerry's skates.

"They used to have skating parties," Tanya said, "when Aunt Lily was a girl. There are skates all over her apartment, all sizes. Makenzie brought up a pair for you."

Skidding and rolling back and forth, they aimed me at a little gold chair. Now I was supposed to get out of the torture shoes and put on these skates. My job was to get these skates on, not to think. Natalie stood back, still breathing hard, waiting for me, hooking her hair behind her ears. She stood there like a picture of a ballet dancer, resting. A painting.

"Do you have room in the toes?" Makenzie wondered. I did. She'd found the right size, but then, Makenzie had always been the best at finding things.

Tanya was on her knees, lacing up my skates for me, tight over my black stockings. Tanya . . . waiting on me? Tanya on her knees before me? I didn't even believe it, but I felt her hands, like birds with rushing wings.

The skittery little chair went over backward when they pulled me to my feet. The skates went in all directions. My legs were trying to do the splits. But they wouldn't let me fall. We moved together now, out onto the ballroom floor like a many-legged thing. All our sequins and satins in a flounce of skirts and peekaboo bra and lace. The glass jewels in our ears and hair flashed the room. And we were on wheels—rattle-trap old unoiled wheels with minds of their own.

"You know what we're like, don't you?" Tanya was saying. "We're like Shannon's cheerleaders." And we were, all trying to make the same coordinated moves and never quite managing it.

Then we started with our scissor-strides, getting up speed. Our skirts strained over our knees. Now we were like elementary school kids at a skating party, playing dress-up. It was that last kids' party of elementary school with all the games that will never work again.

We were the thunder, all around the room, and I felt their hands holding me, overlapping against my back. I didn't have to be clingy, and I was keeping up. They held me. It was the four of us, and who could tell where one of us stopped and the others began? We skated in our clump, getting better at it, swooping with screams around the room, around and around as way out there through the long windows New York began to stir and wake. It was like skating to music, except we were the music.

—◄○►—

"ONCE MORE AROUND," Tanya called out finally. And so we made one last grand turn, circling for a landing. Our skirts brushed the little gold chairs. Our skates raised one final gauzy curtain of dust. I didn't know if I was going to make it. I was wiped out. I couldn't remember when this day started, or yesterday. I almost couldn't remember anywhere but here. Anyone but them.

We dragged our toes and fell into each other. We stopped right where we were meant to. They'd made a little campsite in the enormous room by a pair of French doors onto the terrace. An empty bagel sack and cardboard coffee cups and drained juice bottles stood around. Plastic knives and empty cream cheese tubs. Like a picnic without the blanket, a penthouse picnic. Breakfast? They'd devoured it all, and where was mine? But they couldn't wait.

Then we were settled on the floor in the remains of their breakfast. "We sent Makenzie back to a Starbucks," Tanya said. And I didn't think about where they got the money. Or if they could stick it all on Aunt Lily's bill.

—◄○►—

"We were simply starved," Natalie said. "I don't know how Joanne does it." We were unlacing our skates, yanking them off. Natalie barely made it before she leaned back against the paneled wall and fell gracefully to sleep. Her double lashes fringed her cheeks. An old white skate was still in one of her hands.

The dust settled, gold and now pink in the gray room. "Fairy dust," Makenzie said, and put out her hand. In the next minute she was fast asleep, flat on her back with her arms thrown back, and the glasses still parked up in her spiked hair. And a little cream cheese in the corners of her mouth.

It was just the two of us now, Tanya and me. Like we'd put the children down for their naps. I was ready for mine. So ready. The tiredness, the exhaustion was coming in waves. But slipping down into deep sleep didn't feel all that safe. Somehow I couldn't risk letting those waters close over my head.

I sat hugging my knees, braced against the door frame, one black-stockinged foot out on the terrace. A traffic copter thumped in the air, over there above Central Park. Tanya sat across from me, only a little slumped. She was trying to stay awake too, and succeeding of course. The daylight was finding all the lights in her hair. Her head was heavy, but she was keeping watch. Over me? I felt that gaze of hers that saw right through you to the next thing she wanted.

Were we waiting each other out? Seeing who'd nod off first?

"You and Alyssa at Fabian's?" she said, one of her sudden questions, striking out of the blue. "How did that happen?"

"It just happened," I said. "We were . . . there at the sinks."

"It's a small world," Tanya said.

"Alyssa's in a play on Broadway. She's playing somebody's daughter. She'd taken those two days off to audition. Then she graduated early when she got the part."

"Yes," Tanya said. "Alyssa's quite a little actress." We sat in the doorway, across from each other, like bookends or something. Really just the two of us now, a special . . . privilege.

"And so," I said, "I don't think she was going to have a—"

"Where was Spence?" Tanya asked—another lightning question. "Obviously not in the girls' restroom. But where Alyssa is, Spence can't be far away. Where was he, Kerry?"

Spence. Spence on the train into the city. Spence walking out of the VIP room. I tried to shrug. *The only person standing between Tanya and Spence was Spence,* Alyssa said, in my head. Did Tanya hear that? *Tanya never knew what friendship was,* Alyssa said. *She died not knowing.*

Something panicky was coming up my throat. "I don't know," I said. "I don't know about Spence. I don't think he and Alyssa had anything going particular—"

"In some ways you remind me of me, Kerry," Tanya said in a thoughtful voice. "Though I can't remember being that naive, ever. Not sophomore year. Not ever.

But it doesn't matter now. We know where Spence will be tonight."

—◄○►—

TIME PASSED, AND Tanya let it. The terrace was thick and gritty with New York dirt. The first rays of the sun crept across it, and half of her face was bright, the other shadowed. That place on her forehead that was going to need Botox was darker now. Deeper?

One more second of silence, and I'd be asleep, no matter what. I was worn out with wondering what was real. "Why are we here, Tanya?" I asked her.

"The penthouse?" she said, like that's what I'd meant. She looked past me back into the ballroom. It was like a cave in there now. She ran a hand through her hair. "Every time the market crashes on Wall Street, it's too grand and expensive with too many rooms. People move out," she said. "The old man who built the building back before the Great Depression—1929 or whenever—couldn't sell the penthouse for ages. Aunt Lily's parents had bought her apartment downstairs. She'd come up here to roller-skate with the old man's granddaughters. It was like their own private skating rink. It was empty space for them. Like now."

Jackie and Lee, I almost said. I came this close. I knew Aunt Lily's friends were Jackie and Lee because—

"Jackie and Lee," Tanya said. "And Lee grew up to marry a European prince. And Jackie grew up to marry a President of the United States and became Jackie Kennedy. They were the Bouvier sisters."

They were friends of Aunt Lily's, girlhood friends. The three of them. I knew that because the old woman downstairs had just told me.

And the old woman was Aunt Lily.

It was Aunt Lily, lurking in her own apartment, afraid to be there. Tanya was still looking at me, and through me, reading me. I looked a little above her gaze to that deepening place black on her forehead. Like a darkening star.

She touched it lightly with a finger. "That's where I hit the tree," she said.

"Aunt Lily is downstairs," I said.

I just let go. The words jumped out of my mouth, quicker than an alibi.

Tanya's gaze hardened, focused. You could begin to hear the traffic from down on Seventy-second Street. Rush hour in that world.

"Downstairs? Is she?" Tanya said, only a little interested. "She'd have gone back to Paris after the memorial service. But I can see why she came back. The old busybodies next door, Rhonda Randolph and Flossie. We ran the risk they'd stick their noses into things that didn't concern them. But we had to be somewhere. How do you know this?"

It was one more of her quick questions, like a knife out of nowhere.

"She was there when I went for my things, my backpack, just now."

Tanya nodded. "I sensed . . . somebody in the apartment tonight when we were down there getting our skates and things. Yes, and in the kitchen too when we went in there. Somebody just out of sight. Behind a door, down a hall. Somewhere. Somebody sneaking and creeping. Scuttling like an old crab."

She glanced back across the ballroom to the other door, and my backpack.

I was weighing every word now. "Aren't you afraid she'll tell—"

"She'll be holed up with Rhonda and Flossie," Tanya said. "Adults have their peer groups too, Kerry. And what does it really matter? She's, like, terrified, isn't she?"

"Yes," I said.

"Too terrified to do anything. Besides, what? Call the police? We didn't break in. I had the keys. The doorman gave me the extra set they keep downstairs. The doormen think we're great. They try to hit on us. So who's Aunt Lily going to call? The exterminators? They're just three senile, babbling old women down there. Alzheimer's? It's a real possibility. They've lived too long. Besides, she won't even remember us later. We won't make sense. She can't explain us."

Tanya shrugged and turned her hand over. "Anyway, all that's over now. That time is up. We won't be going back down to the apartment again. We can . . . freshen up in one of the bathrooms up here, before we go."

Go.

I should. Now. Run for my life, wherever that was. I'd said too much already. Tanya could get anything out of you. You'd answer her question, and her eyes would question your answer. And everything would go in a circle, with her at the center. To avoid her eyes, I looked down the slant of morning light falling across Natalie's hand holding the skate. Her long black gloves were off.

Something was wrong with her hand. It wasn't even hers. It was . . . withered and worse. It was shrunken and spotted, greenish. The fingernails were loose. It was almost a claw, oozing something that wasn't blood.

Of course Tanya saw what I was seeing. She could see around corners, around all the corners in my mind.

"Touch her hand."

"No, I don't want to." My hands curled around my knees and hugged them.

"Touch her," Tanya said. "Share a little of your life with her. You won't miss it, and it's only to get her through till tonight. Think about someone else for once, Kerry. For once in your life."

Touch her? Did they need me to—keep them alive? Was that what the roller-skating was about, the touching? I felt their arms around me as we'd pounded around the ballroom floor, around and around. Was I giving them enough life to get through to . . . the next thing Tanya wanted? Was that why I was here?

I uncurled a fist and reached down. It was always just easier to do it. Get it over with. It was always Tanya's way or . . . no way.

On the second try I touched the awful hand that was beginning to rot. Natalie stirred in her sleep, sighed one of her sighs. Her hand slipped away into the folds of her satin skirt, scarlet-red again in the morning sunlight.

Her throat above the dip of the dress and the black of the bra was flawless, swanlike. Natalie.

I didn't want to look at Makenzie. I didn't want to chance it. But she was stretched right there below my elbow. One of her leg-warmer legs was thrown out across one of Natalie's. I made myself look at her sleeping face. My heart thudded, but she was just the same, always the pixie's child, and more of a child while she slept. Except for the glitter on her eyelids and the nightlife spikes of her hair.

Then I smelled it again. The smell of burning, an awful smell of burning flesh.

I'd be sick now, dry-heave sick if I didn't move.

I turned back to Tanya, tried to get it together. "I have to go. I need to get home now."

"How?" she said, looking out into the morning. In profile, she was perfect. Planes were coming in over the West Side, circling for LaGuardia, and she was watching them.

"I'll . . . take a cab to Grand Central."

I waited. For her approval?

"I'm afraid you haven't got the money for a cab," she said, almost to herself. "Breakfast."

Breakfast? Oh. They'd used the money in my backpack for their breakfast. I pictured Makenzie's hand, small and quick, rifling my backpack down in Aunt Lily's dressing room. And then off to Starbucks.

"The subway then," I said. "The number 6."

"I'm afraid we needed all the money," Tanya said, drowsy in the warming sun. "Like every cent, except for two dollar bills we'll be needing in a little while."

The morning narrowed then. Even the ballroom seemed to shrink. "I can walk. Not in those heels. In my flip—"

"All the way home?" Tanya's brow arched high.

My ticket. "My ticket—"

"There was no point in keeping it." She was still gazing out past the edge of the terrace, the parapet. Somehow I could picture the three of them out there, leaning into the night, throwing my ticket away. Somehow I saw it drifting down on Seventy-second Street like a falling leaf. An apple blossom.

I may have been grabbing my new chest, or clutching my throat or something, when Tanya looked back at me. The light was blinding behind her. But then, looking at her had always been like looking into the sun. "Don't dramatize. Don't be a drama queen." She smiled. "Leave the stage work to Alyssa. This isn't a hostage situation. You're not being held for ransom by pirates of the Caribbean."

She was reaching down for the little silver bag she'd carried all evening. "We're all going home tonight, once we've rested up. The four of us. You'll need to be there. Kerry, sometimes I wonder if you know what friendship is. It's not all taking. There comes a time for giving back."

You never know who you'll need, Tanya always said. One of her sayings.

I had to be careful now. But I wasn't used to looking out for myself. As carefully as I could, I said, "If we're not getting home till tonight, I should call—"

"Oh, you want your phone?" Her bag was already in her hand. She snapped it open and fished out my phone. I'd wondered if I'd ever see it again, and there it was. It was almost as if I was supposed to ask for it back. It was almost like part of the . . . script.

"Your mother thinks you're at your dad's, right?" Tanya said. "And I get the idea they don't communicate that well with each other. Messy divorce? Your dad thinks you're with your mother, though frankly I doubt if he gives you that much thought. And so, who are you going to call? What are you going to say?"

I had my phone back—lifeless and useless like anything Tanya didn't need anymore. Who did I think I
was going to call? What would I say? After all, we'd be
there tonight. There.

Where?

We're test-driving these dresses, Tanya had said. *They
need to say "Queens of the Prom and Then Some."* She'd
said that, going into Fabian's.

Sleep was pulling on me now, like something Tanya
wanted.

"We're not going to the prom tonight?" I said to her.
"That's not what this is all about, is it? The prom? How
could we?"

"*We* couldn't," Tanya said patiently. "The prom's the
final senior statement, and you're a sophomore. Sophomores can't go. Unless some senior invited you. And no
senior did. And even then, a senior with a sophomore
isn't in the best of taste. But we might drop by one of the
after-prom parties, where they don't have rules. Maybe
the one at Chase Haverkamp's place. The party the guys
are giving."

How? How could we do that? But it was too big a
question. "And after that?" I said, half dreaming, my
brain going back and forth.

"After that," Tanya was saying, farther off now, "we'll see where the evening takes us."

"But how will we even get there?" My absolute last question before the fog came in.

Tanya was fishing in the little silver clutch, poking around and holding up keys. They gleamed in the sun.

"Aunt Lily's Cadillac," she said. "I'll drive."

CHAPTER NINE

Tanya Time

WE SLEPT THROUGH the day, right where we were, and dreamed. I did. I wondered later if they did, and what they dreamed. The May-time sun climbed the sky. When it was directly overhead, I dreamed of noon standing still, at lunch in the food court, last fall.

The dream was those first days of September when I'd watched them from afar. Tanya's manicured finger moved down her calendar, point by point. I strained to hear what they were saying. I listened hard for clues, but the three of them were faded and too far off.

Natalie sighed, though whether in my dream or there beside me I didn't know. But in one afternoon dream when the light reached all the way across the ballroom floor to our jumble of shoes, I heard the ghostly rumble of roller skates. In the dream here came three girls in old-time skates. Three girls clung to each other, wheels and voices squealing around the corners of the ballroom. Three little girls in funny old-fashioned smocks and Dutch bob haircuts with bows. Three little girls yellow-gray like an old snapshot of themselves. And they had to be Lily and Jackie and Lee.

Then that dream folded like a fan into another one, and here came Tanya and Natalie and Makenzie in roller skates and their prom outfits, skating just the way I'd found them, almost falling but never quite. Makenzie tripping over my backpack.

Then as evening drew on, another dream so dark I almost couldn't see it. A dream of an old lady, bed-ridden with an oxygen tank in a room without air. And a flame-red wig on her head. Rhonda. And bending over her bed, plumping her pillows, was the maid, in Rhonda's spare wig and dark glasses. Flossie. And across the bed from her, Aunt Lily in her bathrobe and her tortoiseshell glasses on a chain, there with them, holed up together, hearing the thunder.

And in all these dreams there were three of them. Always three. Never me.

Somebody just touched my knee, and I rose right out of a dream. I was still braced in the doorway, cramped and gripping my knees. I hadn't moved for hours, and now it was night. Blue velvet night. Tanya hadn't stopped time from passing. Maybe she couldn't anymore.

She was climbing to her feet, brushing off her skirts, being brisk. There below us Natalie and Makenzie were stirring, stiff from the hard floor. The only light was faint and twinkling, from the nighttime glitter city, and I couldn't see Natalie's hands.

We were in the dark, and everything was dimmer than that last dream. And I wasn't as awake as I needed to be. Tanya led us down one hall after another. We padded along in our stocking feet until we found a bathroom with one lightbulb over a green marble sink. The faucets were little gold dolphins.

I watched the three of them around the mirror, repairing their faces with all the swag-bag paint, powder, liner, blush. Brushing their hair with the miniature brushes out of the bags from Chanel and Estée Lauder. Natalie's hands were a blur as she worked over her bejeweled blue-black hair. Expertly. Makenzie edged into the lower half of the mirror to re-glitter her eyelids. They sprayed Arpège and leaned into it. They sprayed and sprayed.

I needed less repair, though a little lip gloss wouldn't kill me. We padded back through the maze of the penthouse to the ballroom where our shoes were. We had to get our feet back into these stilt-heel torture shoes. Mine had the ribbon ties that crisscrossed up the leg.

My backpack was right there, and the flip-flops would feel great, like a . . . walk in the park. But they were out of the question. They didn't say prom night and then some. I thought Tanya would tell me to leave my backpack behind and everything in it.

But when we had our shoes on and our bags on our shoulders, she said, "Don't forget your backpack," and so I took it, and followed them out to the elevator. Following them was what I did best. It was my major.

Time lurched, and now we were in a hurry, on a countdown or something. Tanya's foot tapped as we waited for the elevator. Then we were dropping past thirteen and all the lighted numbers. When had we done this before, in these same clothes? Last night? This year? Sometime. But history wasn't repeating, quite. We were quieter now. Makenzie yawned. Natalie sighed. She'd found her black satin gloves and was working them over her hands, each finger individually.

Now we were teetering and wobbling across the lobby in a cloud of Arpège. Our pointy, spiky shoes rang

on the tiles. Our skirts overlapped. Three or four door-
men were out there at the curb, cupping cigarettes in
the petal-soft spring night. "Give them something to
remember us by," Tanya said over her shoulder.

She did a little something flirty with her skirts as we
turned past them on the sidewalk. Natalie ran a black-
gloved hand down the fall of her hair. Makenzie reached
down to give a leg warmer a little tug. I don't know what
I did. I tried to keep up.

◄○►

THE GARAGE WAS on Seventy-third Street, just off Third
Avenue. A parking valet was instantly there at the end
of the ramp. He was all eyes, looking us over. Taking in
Tanya.

She held up the keys out of her purse. "Miss Garland
wants her Cadillac, please."

"Yikes," the parking guy said. "The boat?"

"Yes," Tanya said.

"It'll take extra time to get it down here," he said. "It
corners like a parade float."

"Do your best," Tanya said.

It took him forever. If Tanya had worn a watch, she'd
be looking at it now. But finally we heard this roar,
and down the ramp came lumbering this enormous

car. Boat? It was the *Titanic.* Huge and black with big drooping, staring headlights. I didn't know how old it was. It had a big toothy front bumper, and fins.

"Full tank?" Tanya said as the valet pushed the gigantic front door open and slid out of the driver's seat.

"Yes," he said, "ma'am."

Tanya handed him two dollar bills. Mine. "I want you up front with me, Kerry," she said, handing my backpack to Makenzie, who was following Natalie into the backseat. They were miles away back there. It was like a hearse.

As I was sliding into the big wheezing leather seat, I remembered the last time Tanya must have been behind the wheel of a car. It crossed my mind, and I reached for the seat belt while we were still parked on the ramp. Tanya found hers. "You two in the back," she said into the rearview mirror. "Buckle up. We don't want to go through all that again."

Then, finding the gear, pumping the brake, Tanya took aim at the street. The car needed a lot of open space to turn, but the rear bumper scraped concrete, and we swayed around into Seventy-third Street.

Then somehow we were on the Ninety-sixth Street approach to the FDR Drive. Who knew how we got there? Park Avenue, I think. Did she have a license? I wondered. *How could she?* I didn't have a license. How could I? I was only—

A horn blasted us as the Cadillac drifted out of our lane into somebody else's. But Tanya fought the wheel. She wasn't perfect, and neither was the Cadillac's steering. But now we were merging with the FDR traffic, then off it and across a river and onto another highway. The traffic was thinning out. Whatever time it was, rush hour was long over. The twinkling high-rises fell back, and the black, leafing-out trees took over.

No sound from the backseat except some light snoring from Makenzie. I tried to look ahead and see myself all the way home, in my room, in bed. But it was too dark out there. I couldn't see a moment ahead, or an inch past the headlight beams on the highway.

I could only steal a glance at the dark line of Tanya's profile, like a silhouette out of black paper. She drove with both hands on the wheel, watching the road, just under the limit. Getting pulled over by the cops was the . . . last thing she wanted. What did I want? If the cops had pulled us over, what would I have done? Said? Would I have run for my life? I doubt it. I doubt it.

But a cop wasn't going to happen because Tanya

didn't want him to. Also, she was being super careful, concentrating on the road too hard for conversation. But after a while, she began to talk, almost to herself, but not really. "I was only a little kid . . . preschool," she said, "when I found out about . . . me."

"What?" I said because I was supposed to.

"You know how little kids try to make the world stop till they get what they want. You know how they yell and scream and throw themselves on the floor and hold their breath."

"I guess," I said.

"I wanted it more," Tanya said. "Whatever I wanted, I wanted it more. You wouldn't believe how long I could hold my breath. I could turn bright blue, and that scared them. My parents. My mother before she went off to Syria and places. My dad, before Joanne. I'd be blue, and they'd think I was dead. Maybe I was.

"And the minute—the *instant* I saw that fear in their eyes, I owned them. You always find your power in other people's weakness. I could bring the world to a stop with what I needed."

"I knew that," I said, in the dark. "Lunch went on too long."

"It went on as long as I said it did. I ruled, and what

else is there? Pondfield Podunk High School? Please. I could have owned the universe with a talent like that. People would rather be ruled than be alone. You of all people should know that, Kerry. Even you. And people will sell you their souls if you'll do their thinking for them. Do you want to study for the exam, or do you want somebody to hand you the answers? Think about it. I could have anything in the world I wanted. And anyone."

She fell quiet, maybe for a mile, thinking about what she might have had. Who.

Spence, I thought. *Spence.*

"But then one day in a single, measly moment," she said, "I looked straight ahead, and instead of all the time in the world and all of it mine, what do you suppose I saw?"

I didn't want to say, but she'd made me see it. "What, Kerry?"

"The apple tree," I murmured.

"Yes." An edge came on her voice, a knife edge. "I was on the phone to you, to join us, if you remember."

"At Nordstrom," I said.

"Nordstrom, wherever," she said. "It was all so totally meaningless, and I missed just that moment. That's the problem with being in charge. The challenge. You can't blink. Ever. The BMW was in the air. Then the tree. And after that awful sound, the car was wrapped around it. You saw the pictures. They were all over the Net. I watched them over and over on my phone."

I'd seen the pictures. But I saw everything now because Tanya was telling it. "I had just time to . . . stop time," she said. "But it was that moment too late. I went over the steering wheel, through the windshield, hit the tree." Her hand came off the Cadillac's steering wheel and touched her forehead.

"This is the part you're not going to understand, Kerry. The part you're so not ready for, but try to keep up. If I could have stopped time in the second before I hit the tree . . . but it was too late, and I couldn't. I broke the windshield, and the windshield broke me. Still, I get what I want, and I wasn't ready to—walk away from my life. I was dead, against the tree in all that bent metal and broken glass and tree bark. I was dead, but it wasn't what I *wanted*. Don't you see that? It wasn't *my decision*. So I was standing beside the car too, just a little safe distance away. By that ditch, in the weeds with my phone still in my hand. The me that matters."

She put her hand out in the dark and touched my

bare arm. I flinched, but it was to show me which me she meant. "Not the ghost of me. Me. The me who doesn't negotiate," she said. "You don't get it, do you? You're not there yet."

No. But somehow I saw it. She made me see it. The soft, sunny Saturday afternoon out on the Country Club Road and the mangled car totaled around the tree like all the pictures. I saw Tanya sprawled there at the end of what had been the hood. The buckled hood. Her head against the apple tree, her forehead . . . embedded. I saw her arms flung out, woven into the branches, and the apple blossoms still falling in her hair. And some blood. Not a lot.

I saw that like a witness on the scene. Then I looked beside the crumpled car, and there Tanya stood, with that mark on her forehead like a dark star, but perfect otherwise. Always the best-looking girl anywhere and the first one you noticed. She stood there with her phone in her hand, and it rang. It was me, trying to call her back, but she didn't have time for that, for me.

"I'd snubbed death like you snub a teacher," she was saying with her eyes on the road. "But this was the first real moment of my life I hadn't shaped for myself. And I couldn't afford another one. I could feel the life leaking out of me. I could feel myself being pulled back toward the car, to the tree. Like . . . undertow."

She needed Natalie and Makenzie, I thought. She had to rule to live.

She heard me knowing that. "I looked all around. Cars were beginning to stop. I found Natalie first, in high grass, farther than I could believe. She'd been in the front seat beside me, where you are now. But then she was way over there in the grass. All arranged, of course, with her purse in her hand. You know Natalie. Not a mark on her. It was like she was just asleep.

"But there was something wrong with the way her head was, like a little crooked on her neck. And I saw she was dead. I came as close to panic as I ever do. 'Natalie, come back here, right now,' I said to her. 'Don't be ridiculous. You've never done a thing on your own, ever. You wouldn't know how. You wouldn't know the first thing about it. You couldn't find the food court without following the crowd.'

"And she opened her eyes and was looking right up at me. Those big violet eyes. Her neck hurt. She put her hand back there. 'Never mind about that,' I said to her. 'We've got to find Makenzie.'

"And when she stood up, the Natalie who'd broken

her neck when she was thrown all that way—*that* Natalie was still there in the grass, perfectly arranged. You know Natalie. She could make even breaking her neck look like the Joffrey Ballet. Natalie reached down and took the purse out of her own hand. Then she tucked her hair behind her ears, and we went looking for Makenzie."

Ahead of the Cadillac, something small with four legs scurried out on the highway. The creature turned its reflector eyes on us, and Tanya tapped the brake. It darted away into darkness.

"We found her right away, facedown in weeds," Tanya said. "She was just then dying. A shudder was going through her. Like a tremor. 'No, you don't, Makenzie,' I said to her. 'Don't even *think* about it. You're—what? Sixteen? You're not going anywhere. You're so totally not ready.'

"I was down on my knees, turning her over. I didn't know how she'd look, but she was perfect too. Not even the beginnings of a bruise. Nothing but grass stains. I think it must have been her heart. She'd slipped away, and her eyes were fixed and staring, so I'd just missed her.

"'No, Makenzie, keep your eyes right here. Right here.'

"'Where?' she said from somewhere down deep—somewhere else. Then she blinked away her dead girl's stare and saw me. She did what I told her to do.

"'Focus,' I said, and she did.

"'Crikey, that was close, wasn't it?' she said in that accent of hers. Then she got up from herself."

We were driving deeper in the dark now. We hadn't met a car for a long time, and I was looking for the turnoff. It was time for the turnoff.

"We brushed ourselves off, and I told them to start walking, away from the road," Tanya said. "Away from the . . . scene. 'And don't run, for Pete's sake. Don't draw attention.' More cars were stopping. People were getting on their phones. Golfers were coming off the course. But we kept walking, and everybody was looking the other way, back at the . . . tree.

"But so what? What if they'd seen the three of us? Nobody knew there'd been three of us in the car. It could have been just me, there on the tree. They didn't find Natalie and Makenzie till later.

"We skirted around the ninth hole of the golf course and just kept going. Natalie's neck was bothering her, but basically she was all right. And she'd hung on to her purse, which was lucky because we'd need train tickets.

"We walked and walked, mostly across yards and parking lots. Parking lots are fine. You could be anybody in a parking lot. Then we were on a sidewalk somewhere. It must have been Hartsdale. We took the train from there. To New York and Aunt Lily's. We had to be someplace."

Tanya flipped the turn signal, and there just ahead, past the massive hood, was the turnoff. Westchester Road, then across the Metro-North tracks and the intersection with Harper Street—Alyssa's street. Then on up to—

"Aren't we there yet?" came Makenzie's voice, half asleep from the backseat. "Aren't we getting close?"

We were. We were coming up to the light at Linden Street. My street. *If the light was red and we had to stop, I could snap myself out of the seat belt and—*

But the light was green. It *would* be for Tanya. We gunned on up the hill, through the sleeping town. Nobody'd be up at this hour except for the after-prom people. Everybody else would be safe at home.

"I don't know how I did it," Tanya said quietly. "But I'm not surprised I did. They rose up because I said so— Natalie and Makenzie. I raised them from the dead."

CHAPTER TEN

Where the Evening Took Us

THE GATES OF the Haverkamp estate stood open, and the gatehouse glowed. Gas torches flamed up in the dark. Big, billowing silk flags flanked the gates. One flag in blue and silver, Pondfield High colors. The other in Harvard red—crimson—because Chase Haverkamp had gotten in there. The road was lined with cars. SUVs were pulled off on the shoulders.

We crept past the front gates in the hulking Cadillac. Only a few stragglers were walking up the private drive to the house. Late arrivals to the A-list party.

Tanya drove on past more cars and turned up a little side street, deeper into darkness. Up here all the lights were out in the McMansions, except for the little pin-point gleams from the security systems, like sequin stars.

She pulled in under a tree. When she shut off the engine and killed the lights, my seat belt felt tighter. I was having trouble breathing. But I didn't have to meet her gaze in the inky night. I couldn't see the arch of her eyebrows.

"Why are we doing this?" I said. "How can you go to the party? You can't."

"No." One of her hands seemed to rest on the bottom of the big metal steering wheel. "But you can, Kerry. That's what you're for."

"I don't want to," I said, though when had whining ever helped? "I want to go—"

"It doesn't matter what you want, Kerry. It never has. There's something you've forgotten. You have a very convenient memory, even for somebody your age. Try to remember."

I sat there, strapped down by the seat belt. She'd hear if I tried to unsnap the clasp, make a run for it. In these heels? I tried to remember what I was supposed to remember. Maybe if I did, she'd let me—

"The phone call, Kerry—when I called you . . . from

the car. If you'd picked up on the first ring like you should have, maybe—just maybe none of this would have happened. Maybe you wouldn't have our blood on your hands."

"But I—"

"But you didn't pick up on the first ring. You don't know the first thing about responsibility. About what you owe other people. But tonight's the night you learn."

I was numb now, all over, and she owned me. She owned every corner of my mind.

Then just as Tanya was unfastening her seat belt, Makenzie said—suddenly from the backseat—"She's gone."

Just those two words.

We were both out of our seat belts and heaving open the huge, heavy old car doors, Tanya and I. There was nowhere to run now. I couldn't find my feet, in the ditch, in the dark. The dome light inside the car was on, making everything outside blacker than before.

Tanya was yanking open the back door on her side, the street side. I was pulling on the back door on mine. Makenzie was jammed against it, as far from Natalie as she could get. Now she tumbled out and was clutching me, clinging. I could feel her hands all over me, and we were staggering in a ditch. Doing this dance.

The dome light was ghastly, glaring, and Natalie was sprawled against the big overstuffed backseat. And for the first time ever, there was nothing graceful about her. She still wore her gloves. I saw that and I was glad about it. Relieved or something. The red satin of her dress glared back at the dome light.

Her head had fallen forward, Natalie's. It hung down from her broken neck.

"Natalie," Tanya said, but there was something hopeless in her voice, so it wasn't quite Tanya. "Natalie, come—" She was reaching into the car with both hands, to take Natalie by her satin shoulders, give her a shake. Natalie's head lolled back against the seat in the awful light.

And she had no face.

Her hair was tucked, smooth and blue-black, behind her ears. But she had no face. I can't tell you more. I can't tell you more than that. She'd been dead for weeks.

And the satin of her dress was settling against— nothing. Bones, maybe. Maybe not even bones. But not Natalie.

She was dead. This was real. I staggered, blind and

crazy, but I wasn't going anywhere. Where do you go in a nightmare? Makenzie had me in a grip, stronger than I could believe.

"She couldn't help it," Makenzie whispered in a rushed way against me, against my sequined front. "Natalie couldn't. She'd stayed as long as she could. We all stayed as long as we could."

The spikes of Makenzie's hair brushed my face, and that hideous smell of burning—burning flesh—cut my eyes and filled the night. That suffocating smell that I breathed in before I could stop myself.

I pried her off me, and pushed her as hard as I could back onto the car seat. I got rid of her, but I could still feel the clutch of her hands on my bare arms. And the smell of her on me. *That* smell. It was a coffin inside the car now, where I pushed her. It always had been—a tufted, overstuffed coffin, with ashtrays. I wouldn't look. I couldn't. Besides, the car was full of swirling smoke now, cremation smoke. Makenzie was smoldering. And that death smell, all mixed up with Arpège and apple blossom.

I whirled around, ready to run now, even if I broke both legs. Even if I ran off the edge of the world. I was gasping for air. And there—right in front of me in the dark—was Tanya. Somehow she was on this side of the smoking car, with something in her hand. Tanya there, between me and . . . escape.

Chalky pale in the smoky light, dark-starred Tanya. It was my backpack she was holding.

"They're gone," she said. "I'm going. It won't be long now."

Go now, I said, inside my head. I was screaming in there. *Go now and leave me in—*

"I only have minutes more," she said. "That's as far as the evening will take me."

Only minutes. But you couldn't trust Tanya with time.

"It's party time," she said.

—◄○►—

AND YOU COULD hear it behind her in the dark, the sounds of the after-prom party. There in the distance the clink and babble and splash of an A-list party around a pool.

"Don't worry," Tanya said, looking right through me to the next thing she wanted. "I only need to say good-bye to Spence. It'll be fine. It'll be fun. He won't even remember it later. It won't make sense, so he'll think somebody spiked his drink or something. He won't remember a thing."

We were walking in the dark now, away from the street and the Cadillac. She didn't even have to hold on to me. Not with her hand. It was my backpack in her hand.

She was sure-footed enough for both of us. She was part of the dark. We were between houses, drifting through a scent of lilac, that clean spring scent. She knew the way. She so knew the way.

Another path around a garden shed, another gate, and we were in the grounds of the Haverkamp estate, the back way in. Gardens like rooms with high hedges for walls and the starry sky for a ceiling. Very French, like Versailles or someplace.

And through the openings in the hedges the party pulsed and strobed. People in the pool and strings of colored lights above a crowded terrace. A band, blaring, and people dancing, their hands pointing out the stars. People making their final senior statement.

We stood, shadowed by the hedge in the empty garden. In the center was a lily pond, round as a big silver coin, catching the drifting moon.

"Go get Spence," she said in my ear. My rhinestoned

ear. "Bring him to me. I only need that moment. It's the least you can do."

"What if I can't find—"

"He's right there."

He was. Right there beyond the walled garden, framed by an opening in the hedge. This side of the glowing turquoise pool. You could see his blondness and the white blur of his shirt. The moon was out. All the guys had shed their tux coats. They were in shirtsleeves. Their ties were loose. Cool. Keeping it real.

"Get him," Tanya said in a fading voice.

I waited. I tried to wait her out, to stall. Maybe she might just . . . go now. This minute. But of course time wasn't going to run out until she'd said good-bye to Spence. I saw that. She'd made me see that.

So I turned on the glittering gravel of the path. I couldn't feel my feet in these torture shoes. And why hadn't I broken a heel by now? I didn't want to do this, but it was just easier to do what she wanted. Get it over with. I took one step, and the night exploded.

A terrible, erupting sound bounced off the night. Birds rose in clouds out of the trees, birds black against dark blue. Only the blaring band muffled the sound for the party people. I didn't know what it was, not at the time. How could I? It was the Cadillac, ablaze. And the flames had reached the gas tank. It went off like a bomb and burned down to a rusty frame.

I whirled around, not knowing this, not knowing what that sound meant. And my backpack was at Tanya's feet. And in her hand the longest knife off the wall of Aunt Lily's kitchen. The knife that had come all this way in my backpack.

Tanya was nearer now, half out of the shadow. The moon caught all the pale lights in her hair. But her forehead was darker than night now. Darker and deeper.

"If only you hadn't looked back," she said in a voice not faded at all. "But then you never could get anything quite right, could you, Kerry? Now I'll have to go get Spence myself. You didn't really think I'd leave him behind, did you? For Alyssa? Please."

The knife flashed in her hand, quick as one of her questions. The moon struck blue fire off it. She was going to kill Spence. And me too. I was in her way, and she had no more use for me. I'd seen the knife. I knew too much. I'd gone from not knowing anything to knowing too much.

This was either the last moment of my life, or the first. I needed the knife. And had one second to get it.

Not even. And this time it had to be my time. For the first time.

She was swooping to slash. I grabbed her wrist and caught her by surprise. We were both surprised. Who did I think I was? The knife was turning and turning between us. She was stronger than I was. She always had been, in every way, and she still was. And there was all this life in her.

And I'd never been in a fight with anybody, not even in middle school. But I sank my nails into her wrist, and the knife jumped out of her hand. We tripped each other up and were both on the ground now, tangled in our skirts, ripping the knees out of our stockings, groveling in the gravel, grabbing for shadows that might be the knife.

Then I had it. Don't ask me how. It was in my hand, and I had it against her throat. I was up in a crouch over her, and she was on her back, and the point of the knife was against her throat. Some other me had her by the throat.

I couldn't kill her. She was already dead. But I could send her—speed her on her way, without Spence. Or me. I shouldn't have to die. I'd never lived. I'd only followed.

She made a little move, and I jabbed the knife. It must have broken the skin. She must have felt a line of blood run down her, into the scoop neck of her leotard. She never spoke, saving her strength. She never moved again, waiting for me to blink. Playing for time.

How long? And all in silence now, except for the siren of the fire engine whining in the distance, looking for the Cadillac. The band had stopped blaring, and the birds in their clouds never came cawing back. How long until there were silver edges on the shadows?

Daylight was coming, and I could see the line of black blood that had run down her. And I saw her eyes, watching mine. She wasn't looking through me to the next thing she wanted. She saw me.

"The party's over," I told her.

And there seemed to be no more need for the knife. Her eyes were still staring, but not at me.

I heaved myself up on my feet, stiff as a board and cold to the bone. I walked over to the lily pond and had to pry the knife out of my hand. I threw it in the water.

That must be the quietest time there is, that silver-gray time before real daylight.

Then from behind me I heard a sound. A shoe scraped gravel. A sound of shaking leaves and the crackle of branches. I heard her behind me . . . Tanya. And I didn't have the knife anymore. The pond was all lily pads, overlapping, and the knife was nowhere.

I didn't know which way to run, and now one of the heels of my shoes had broken off, finally. I couldn't run. I spun back to where we'd been there on the ground, where I'd held her on the point of the knife.

And she wasn't there.

She was hanging on the hedge. Her head—her face was embedded in all that spiky, prickly greenness. Her arms were flung out, woven into the branches. Like the apple tree out by the Country Club Road. Her body hung there. *She* was gone. Then not even her body. I saw the mismatching skirts settle against nothing and droop down the leafy hedge.

I stood there in the silver-gray morning, all on my own.

CHAPTER ELEVEN

Sunday Morning

THE SUN SLANTED across me, all the way down through town. Sunday morning, with church bells tolling. I walked down the curving roads and then the straight streets. Past empty porches and swing sets and front walks bordered in masses of pink and white flowers. Everything hemmed with golden sunlight and dew on the lawns like a billion diamonds. I'd never been this awake this early.

Downtown, I walked a block out of my way, to the thrift shop. "Second Act" or "Encore." Some name like that. You weren't supposed to leave donations out- side the door when it wasn't store hours. But I left my backpack there, and they could take it or leave it. Inside were my Fabian's clothes—the slinky skirt, the sequin top, the broken shoes. And another pair of strappy shoes and two mismatching skirts and a leotard, a little stained.

I was back in my school clothes from . . . when? Friday? My American Apparel sweatshirt was tied in a knot around my waist.

I turned away from my bulging backpack, and a car pulled up at the curb. The only car in sight. Spence Myers at the wheel, leaning out of his dad's Acura. Spence Myers, one of the rare seniors who could get away without owning his own car. Except he wasn't a senior now. He'd graduated. Had I?

"You again." Spence propped an elbow out of the car window. And he was grinning because there I was again, this time disguised as myself.

"You again," I said. I wanted to smooth my hair—do something with it. But that was Natalie, not me.

"It's got to be fate," Spence said.

I laughed. I doubted it, but I laughed.

"What are you doing out this early?" he said.

"Just running an errand." I nodded back at the thrift shop.

"Me too." He jerked a thumb at the backseat. Two other senior guys were back there, Ben Chou and Grant Carmichael, in their tux shirts, curled up and sound asleep. Zonked.

"You the designated driver?" I asked him.

"That's me," Spence said. "Eagle Scout to the end. But they're not going to Georgetown, so I'm not stuck with them forever."

"Was it a good party?" I said.

"You weren't there, were you?"

"You could hear it all over town."

"It was good," Spence said. "Same old crowd, but saying good-bye this time. Letting go and moving on."

We made that sunny morning moment last, though I'd never be able to tame time like Tanya. But I was there on the curb, and Spence was leaning out of the car, and it ought to be awkward, but it wasn't.

"I'll e-mail you from Georgetown," Spence said. "Tell you all about it."

"Sure you will," I said, grinning.

"No, really. And hop in. I'll drive you home. Plenty of room up front."

"It's okay," I said. "I'm practically there."

So he nosed the Acura out into the street, doing his

designated-driver thing. His take on community service. And I peeled off toward home, not wanting to show up in his rearview window, watching him go. And just now remembering that he and I were both here and alive, breathing in this morning, because of me.

I headed on down Linden Street in my flip-flops. I had my phone, so I called my mom.

◄○►

THE DOOR TO our apartment was standing open, and she was there in the hall. Fuzzy slippers. Bathrobe. But she'd been up for a while. She didn't look mad. Relieved, yes. And maybe curious.

She breathed in. "Arpège? That's a blast from the past," she said, "and are those diamonds in your ears?"

"What? Oh." I reached up and took off the rhine-stone earrings, which really didn't go with anything. "No. They're not real."

"You weren't at your dad's," she said. But it wasn't like she was accusing me.

"No," I said. "I was nowhere near him."

"He's not that easy to get near," she said with a small shrug. A coffee smell drifted out of our kitchen. Yes, she'd been up awhile.

"Where were you an hour ago?" she said.

An hour ago?

Then I knew, to the very minute. That was when I was turning back from the lily pond, to . . . the hedge.

"Why?" I said.

"I was in bed," my mom said. "I hadn't slept, but an hour ago I knew I'd get you back."

"How?"

She turned up her hands. "I'm your mother. Are you going to tell me about it?"

"Yes," I said, "when I'm an old woman and you're a *really* old woman."

"I can wait." She smiled a small smile. "We've got the time."

Then—right then, in my pocket—my phone rang. It rang and rang. I let it.

About the Author

Described by *The Washington Post* as "America's best living author for young adults," Richard Peck is the first children's book writer ever to have been awarded a National Humanities Medal. His extensive list of honors includes the Newbery Medal (for *A Year Down Yonder*), a Newbery Honor (for *A Long Way from Chicago*), the Edgar Award (for *Are You in the House Alone?*), the Scott O'Dell Award (for *The River Between Us*), the Christopher Medal (for *The Teacher's Funeral*), and the Margaret A. Edwards Award for lifetime achievement in young adult literature. He has twice been a finalist for the National Book Award. Mr. Peck lives in New York City.